SMOKETOWN

Tenea D. Johnson

SMOKETOWN

TENEA D. JOHNSON

Blind Eye Books
blindeyebooks.com

Smoketown
by Tenea D. Johnson

Published by:
Blind Eye Books
1141 Grant Street
Bellingham, WA 98225
blindeyebooks.com

Edited by Nicole Kimberling
Cover art by Sam Dawson
Interior Art by Dawn Kimberling

First edition July 2011
Copyright 2008 by Tenea D. Johnson-
Printed in the United States of America.

ISBN 978-0-9789861-5-5

1

Anna Armour had had her fair share of failed resurrections. There had been the lichen when she was three and the dragonfly at six—the sad twisted platypus that her mother took away before it ruined her tenth birthday. Since the day of her mother's death when Anna was fourteen, she hadn't brought anything to life.

Now, she only wanted to bring someone back to her, but this feat proved the most elusive. Sixteen years of ignoring that part of herself had paid off though: She had traded her secret gift for a well-honed endurance. So no matter how tired Anna became she always carried her determination and her regret.

Even now, after working a double shift, she picked up her pace as she crossed the street in a throng of other warehouse workers. The strap of her pack, heavy with Peru's package, dug into her shoulder. Anna hooked one thumb under the strap and lifted it momentarily to ease the strain. But she never slowed her gait. She didn't want to miss the last train to the post office before the long holiday break.

Looking up from the crowded street, she saw the glint of the 16:37 train reflecting sunlight as it rounded the last curve before it reached the station. It was six minutes early. Anna took off running.

A shifting maze of people stood between her and the train station. She tried to pick a path, dodging people as best she could. Her pack bounced against her tailbone. Anna excused herself as she twirled around her supervisor. The entrance to the train station glowed in front of her, the overhead giene lights brighter even than the sunlight shining on the sidewalk. She squinted against the glaring lights as she hit the stairs. Taking them two at a time, she pulled on the banister with each stride, propelling her body forward.

At the top of the stairs, she nearly collided with a young man, knocking his shoulder back so hard that for an awkward second he seemed to be dancing. Anna yelled apologies over her shoulder and focused on the approaching train. The smooth silver of its cylinder turned matte black as it entered the station. The train slid silently to a stop, the door opening as it came to rest. She slowed to a trot and hopped over the lip of the threshold. In two strides she swung the bag around to her front, lowered her weight onto the nearest seat and strapped in.

It was cold inside the train. The air conditioning chilled the sweat on her brow and she suppressed a shiver. Across from her hung a transit map. It showed the circles of Leiodare's rail system as well as the distant outlines of the other city-states that lay beyond the surrounding jungle. She chuckled quietly looking at it. The scale of the maps in Leiodare was always off—as if it were the largest city-state in the southeastern US when it clearly wasn't, perhaps the third largest at best. But inside the city that didn't matter. As the train zipped further down the line, Anna looked above the map to the time glowing blue. Seventeen minutes till close; she should just make it.

At the post office, battalion members stood sentry at a new security gate just outside the entrance. Anna joined the short line, shaking her head imperceptibly. The gate made no sense. Though Leiodaran paranoia dictated that people should be searched as they left the post office, even the city's unstable framework of beliefs couldn't make sense of examining people as they entered the post office. No one smuggled contraband to the outside world; Leiodare was the city surrounded by an invisible fence after all.

But in the short time she'd been in Leiodare, Anna had noticed that around the outbreak's anniversary, all manner of new and exotic municipal neuroses took hold. Last year, there had been talk of elevating the all-encompassing barrier further into the city's airspace. Only the cost had quieted that particular fervor. So this year she supposed they'd decided to erect the ominous red gates outside all the post offices and ports of entry.

Anna clenched her jaw as she looked around, waiting for the woman in front of her to enter the security gate. After that woman had passed inspection, the battalion member on the right waved Anna through.

As she stepped across the red threshold, a shrill alarm sounded.

Anna froze, her hands already up to protect herself. The battalion guards pushed past her, running to the bank of post office boxes near the exit, weapons drawn. Their boots sent flowers flying as they crossed the grassy median and joined a circle of other soldiers whose attentions were trained on the ground. Anna could see a man stretched out there, with hands behind his head.

She rushed through the gate and into the post office.

Standing at the counter she wondered what the man had done. Had it been a false alarm or had he been so stupid as to try and smuggle birds through the post? Everyone knew that Leiodare had outlawed birds twenty-five years ago. The city was infamous for it. No birds could be found in the city's beautiful gardens, on its houses, or in its trees. Smugglers, and often even suspected smugglers, served no less than five years of hard labor maintaining the electric avian barrier that surrounded the city, stretching into the sky, and across Leiodare, just below the path of planes. She couldn't imagine what price could tempt someone to risk that sentence. But Anna knew, perhaps better than most, that people did crazy things for paltry rewards.

She removed the package from her bag and placed it on the automated belt in front of her. The warm yellow light of the autoscan briefly illuminated its contents: the notched circle of an ancient viewfinder reel and chunks of unrefined crystal rock.

"Invalid addressee," the autoscan belched back.

"Override for correction." Anna spoke quietly. This always happened. "Peru, person, not Peru, location. Shipping location is Mail Depot 92-G. Confirm with sender shipping history."

As she waited for the autoscan to locate the records, she inserted a receiving slip into the other side of the machine so she could pick up a package of her own. In seconds, the belt brought up a matchbox-sized parcel with a small barcode printed onto the outside. Anna grabbed it and placed it into her pack. She continued to wait for her package to Peru, her gaze traveling over it. As always, Anna had written her return address in exaggerated, long block letters, spelling it crookedly so that Peru would recognize her hand.

The autoscan finally chimed its acceptance and the belt clicked on, moving the package into the recesses of the post office, and hopefully closer to Peru. If not, perhaps the package she had received could close the gap.

Anna waited till she arrived at home to open it. There, she stood at the high kitchen counter, looking down at the package. The virtu real inside, red and small as a quarter, held her hopes. If Peru had been the virtuoso who made the real, she would be able to tell by the frequency, the feel of the real, and then because she knew where the real had come from, she'd have some clue as to where Peru was living. Every real had a neurological signature and Anna knew Peru's nearly as well as her own. She removed her virtu rig from the kitchen drawer and placed the darkened glasses over her eyes. She made sure to line the 'trodes up with the proper points on her skull and slipped the real inside the loading door at the temple. She pressed the load button and hit "Play."

Instantly, a sea of sands stood in front of her, perhaps somewhere in Idaho, she supposed. Heat radiated up from the ground in visible waves. The perspective turned and looked down at a small pool of water. It inched closer to the water, and to Anna's disbelief she saw the face of the person recording the real. The virtuoso wore the standard virtu's darkened aviator glasses that were part of every virtu rig, but below them Anna saw a caramel-skinned woman with full lips and high cheekbones. The woman actually smiled and waved into the pool of water.

Anna jerked the rig off in disgust. Amateur! A virtuoso never showed her face in a real—perhaps if it had been ordered custom, but never on a general disc. Everyone knew that. It was the first thing Peru had taught her about recording reals and even as a formerly sheltered kid of fourteen Anna had never made that mistake. No chance it was Peru.

How would she ever find her? Anna had been two years in this city, waiting for Peru, or rather trying to bring Peru to her. Anna believed staying in Leiodare was her best chance of reuniting with Peru because Leiodare's lucrative virtu assignments would have beckoned to her. And Anna still remembered the rapture on Peru's face as they sat, watching the travel advertisements for Leiodare while they rode down the River Ruelle, ferrying from their last home to the next.

Peru insisted on calling every place home. She said otherwise they would be lost, and as much as Peru loved the dark, she despised the feeling of being lost in it. But with each passing month Anna's doubts grew.

She could tell it would be a dreading night. To calm herself, she decided to draw.

Anna sat down in a corner of her apartment, sketchbook on her lap as she leaned over and tried to think of what to draw. Tinny music from her downstairs neighbor switched on and floated up through the floorboards. The bass vibrated the tiny cymbals that he sold on holidays. Some of Anna's other drawings, half-finished faces formed in graphite, covered the floor immediately around her.

Two corners of the apartment were lit; the rest dim as always, awash only in the faint amber lighting from the distant Spires. A single drawing lamp dangled down from the ceiling. Opposite the lamp, a bay window dominated the short west wall. Light poured in from it and melded with the bright yellow light emanating from the giene spa.

Tonight the graphite didn't satisfy her. The lines were too fine—not just for the dark, but for her mood. She grabbed a pack of charcoals she'd found in a damaged shipment at the warehouse. The charcoal had looked promising when she'd discovered it. Each piece was wrapped in soft red paper, and as she opened the top and tore the paper halfway down, the charcoal itself was revealed. It looked to be drop black—a soft, expensive, dense black—of a quality rarely seen by picker/packer girls like her, living on blue grains and memory. The charcoal felt warm and right in her hands, an unspoken desire satisfied.

Angling the pad closer, she began to draw. With the first motion of her wrist, the char marked so deeply it seemed to create a space in the paper. She drew her next-door neighbor with deep shades of drop black. Anna sketched the hollows of her face, the ferocity of her eyes, the wrinkles that spoke of years she would never share. She drew the morning callers. Though the charcoal muted their colorful robes, it kept the beauty of her favorite caller's jawline, the strength of her chin, the richness of her face.

When she'd finished the drawings, Anna straightened and stretched slowly, grunting past the aches and pains the warehouse had left in her. She walked over to the other bright corner of the loft and hung the portraits inside the small giene spa where light poured down in cleansing ultraviolet. The light was a luxury she could never afford, but one required by law. Days before she moved in, workmen had hurriedly affixed the bank of UV lights and installed the wash stall—thus converting the old bathroom into a proper giene spa. Feeling the beginnings of exhaustion creep up, Anna crossed the room to her bed and lay down.

The birds were an afterthought: a last late-night flash as she was already sinking into dreams. The vision of the swans came to her there, in the in-between. Two tiny cygnets, downy and light grey in their youth, glided across the river where she and Peru had spent a spring harvesting butterflies for traveling money. While Peru picked up their pay, Anna sat on the bank of the river, watching as the two orphan cygnets floated on the current. Despite her fatigue, Anna wanted to draw this last image before going to sleep. She rolled over and reached for the sketchbook. She leaned against the wall, her legs still under the covers, the pad stretched out before her, a clean new page shining and the drop black already staining her fingers. The image of two birds came quickly, not drawn so much as surfaced from the black she'd surrounded them with. Charcoal covered nearly the whole page.

The birds' bills were black; their eyes were of it, but the rest of them, their sweet soft bodies, were the only white left on the page. They radiated off of it. They seemed soft enough to touch. Her fingers hovered above the birds, wanting to feel them without smudging the image. As she held her hand there, something tickled the center of her palm. Tingling spread across her hand. When she moved it back, her finger touched something hard—the tip of a black bill.

Anna stared down at a small cygnet. It perched on the paper in her lap, watching the space to its left. The second swan rose from the sketchpad as smoothly as if an elevator had brought it to where it and its companion stood, staring up at her.

"Shit," Anna cursed quietly.

At moments like this, turning moments she called them, thoughts didn't work. They got stuck somewhere in the back of her mind, and a feeling, usually something between wonder and nausea took over. If she was lucky that was all. Cursing was her attempt to begin to think again. Sometimes it worked. This time it didn't, but it felt good to say. She stared down at her steady hands, felt a slow, quiet warmth spill into her chest and tried to recognize the feeling—not wonder, not nausea, not—.

One of the cygnets took a step closer; its down brushed her hand.

Anna's brain lurched back into motion, shot out a few more choice expletives, then stopped, stalled by her realization.

"Shouldn't be possible," she whispered. As she watched the birds in her lap, it was relief, still and steady that spread through her. Of all things, relief.

"Shit. Shitting. Shit it," she said. She looked away, trying to think. Her gaze traveled up the wall of window across from her. Her reflection was bright and clear against the black glass. It sat in a circle of light, the covers around her dappled with charcoal dust. She'd left a streak of it on her jaw without noticing. It stood out on her skin, part of it obscured by the black spirals of hair that radiated out from her head and brushed her shoulders. Beyond her reflection, the brightness of the distant Spires lit up its section of Leiodare.

Anna focused past the image of herself and onto the city. Already the night looked lighter, as if dawn were a short nap away and here she sat, a crime on her lap and unleashed power in her hands.

2

The first day Anna kept her distance from the cygnets, but by the second she couldn't ignore their small sounds of hunger and began to feel silly for being afraid of two fluffy baby birds. Anna spent all her time with them. She picked them up and examined them against information she found online. They looked the same as the cygnets in the files that she found. They acted as the articles said that they should. Even if she knew they weren't natural she couldn't find any difference between them and all the other birds she'd encountered before moving to this city. In fact they seemed even more harmless with their downy grayish bodies and inquisitive stares.

The holidays started the next day so Anna had to go back to work. The holidays that commemorated the Crumble outbreak and quarantine had no official name. Some called it the Mourning; Anna, like the outsider she was, preferred Death Days. By whatever name, they were holidays and, normally, she would never miss the triple-time pay that came with working on them. It was the only thing anyone at the warehouse knew about her, so she needn't call attention to herself by not showing up.

Just before her shift started, she finished soundproofing the giene spa. She activated the spa's warming ultraviolet and filled the gentle jet tub with water for the cygnets to swim in. As she watched them float she felt satisfaction. They had now reached some approximation of a workable habitat and for all her hard work, the swans rewarded her by acknowledging her existence, swimming towards her, up to the rim of the tub. For that she felt unexpectedly delighted as she watched from the doorway.

Reluctantly, she gathered her things and left the apartment to rejoin the rest of the city.

Leiodare the Lit, they called it. Its founders had given it a new name to divorce it from Middlesboro's history, or rather its messy transition from Kentucky farmland to jungle and the environmental upheaval that had caused it. It worked. Leiodare shone like an oasis of radiance amongst the dark hills that encircled it—a tiny bowl at the bottom of a jungle mountain range that had captured all the surrounding beauty. Before the short-lived Crumble outbreak and quarantine, travelers and natives alike treasured Leiodare. They spent their extra money and their time to bask in its glow.

Back then, birds roosted in its perches, and monkeys mated in the massive gardens that bisected one side of the city from the other. Their calls had floated through Leiodare, as much a trademark of the city as the twenty-first-century Revival architecture and carnivale festivals that filled the streets. A *Times* journalist had once famously written that if the tobacco farmers and holler people of the past could see what would become of their birthplace, they might have blown the place to smithereens long before climate change transformed it.

Train tracks surrounded the city center on blue-lit rails, ferrying passengers from spired skyscrapers in the Heart to nightclubs in The Shallows while they stared out the windows, hoping to catch a glimpse of a baby macaque. At night, fireflies and the bulbous bioluminescent lights of flaren dotted the trees in the parks, flashing pinpoints of red, blue, and purple. Their tiny lights created a place to rest the eyes when myriad carnivale commandeered the streets at regular intervals. And in the vast brownstone businesses that lined McClaren Street, you could find an original vinyl of Prince as easily as a tart if you knew which stoop to ascend. Those who knew and those who aspired to know, had renowned Leiodare as a place of possibility, pleasure, and sophistication.

Much had changed in the last twenty-five years.

What was once the Heart was now only the Center. Though much of the city's beauty had persevered, these days, pinpoints of light danced in the Leiodaran dark for other reasons.

Flames from thousands of candles swayed with the collective breath of the city. Most of its inhabitants assembled on McClaren Street for the unfestive holiday, the marking of March twenty-seventh—the day that the last infected died, the last body burnt, a few months before the quarantine was lifted, and birds were declared illegal.

Red candles covered the stoops of McClaren Street. They dotted the sidewalks and dominated the windowsills, the rooftops, and stairs. One candle burned for each person who had perished during the three months that Leiodare was shut away from the rest of the world. There were no candles for those left behind, or even for the friends who had had to sever ties when supplies ran low and monkeys were hunted like rabbits. And certainly not for the birds that had been exterminated. One in four humans died during the quarantine. Ninety percent of the bird population had perished, most at the hands of the people who had once taken no more notice of them than of the clouds overhead.

These people and their descendants, the ones on the street in their light jackets and heavy thoughts, stood gazing into the candlelight, a spectacle as beautiful as the celebrations of the time before—simpler, quieter perhaps but just as memorable. They did their civic duty, took care of themselves—not so much each other—and quietly lived in fear. Such was Leiodaran culture, twenty-five years after the city had been abandoned by the outside and left to its own devices. Back then, the borders had only been closed for three months, but Leiodare had turned during its time alone.

Fresh off her shift, Anna skirted the perimeter of the crowd. It stood between her and her building. Near her, a gaggle of others, mostly other non-natives she assumed, kept up running conversations. She watched the ceremony with disquiet as she thought of the birds upstairs. In the distance, she could still hear chants from the protestors cordoned a block away in Lumpur Park. Anna looked toward the distant corner where animal rights activists and Starling gang members had been thrown together by their mutual ire for the commemoration. The animal rights activists tried to create some space between themselves and the Starlings but to no avail. A few activists watched the Starlings nervously from the edges of the crowd. The Starlings didn't frighten Anna. To her, the gangs seemed just another distraction for an anxious generation looking for a way to take their mind off the weather and how much habitat would be left as they aged—same as everywhere in North America and, she expected, everywhere else.

Now the protestors were chanting, but earlier it had been nearly the whole city. Even inside the warehouse during work she had heard it. The sound of finger cymbals could be lost in the forklift's engines and the whirr of the carts as she and a few other pickers rolled around the warehouse's wide aisles. But the chanting had been inescapable. One couldn't get away from the feeling of one hundred thousand people chanting in unison. The vibration had ran up her spine, rattled her.

Leiodare's holy days had always disturbed Anna: the chanting, the candles, the scarecrows, and the cleansing ceremonies. Because she wasn't a native, most of Leiodaran culture intrigued her, but not these three days in the winter when all the city seemed in a fever. She had spent all day wanting only to go home and check on the cygnets, to make sure she hadn't hallucinated the reintroduction of magic back into her life.

Now the crowd stood between her and them. In her backpack, courtesy of a stop at the pet depot, thirty flies wrapped up in a plastic bag like goldfish lay in the bottom of the pack, and though this was no crime in itself, Anna thought it best that that she get inside.

Given the size the crowd, she knew it would be a challenge. Amazing that she could forget how many people gathered on this single street. The spectacle had dumbfounded her during her first year here, but now thoughts of the cygnets kept her focused. She looked for pockets of space in the crowd, trying to chart a course through the swell of people who clogged the entrance to her building. Anna turned back to the center of the street. A flash of green fabric stood out in the crush of people. Seeing it, Anna decided to stay, and not because of the trudge through the crowd. By the look of the group of fans dressed in small green capes she wasn't the only one focused on something other than the commemoration. They, and she, stayed for the calls, or more specifically, the caller.

At the center of the street, on a raised platform alongside a griot from the historical society, stood Anna's favorite morning caller. Anna found the woman's voice remarkable. It hovered between suggestive and refined. Each morning she heard her song-like calls rise up over the din of traffic, bend around buildings and charm Anna into dreams.

Anna momentarily rose up to her tiptoes, focusing on her. As always, the caller wore a jade green robe with a large hood and enormous bell sleeves. It completely obscured her body and most of her face, leaving just her jaw and mouth visible. The hood overhung, concealing the rest of her features. It revealed full lips though, plum against the rest of her face's deep brown complexion. Her lips stood out against the green, drawing Anna's eye. From what Anna could see, she looked to be a younger woman, not much older than Anna's thirty years. The rest of the crowd, no doubt, noticed the robe's shimmer more than anything else.

The robe had been constructed of the rare peacock floss sold in The Shallows and reputed to be manufactured from the last remnants of the gossamer bushes that had once attracted butterflies and bolds to the center of the city. Anna had seen images of the immense white birds hovering over the bushes, butterflies lighting across the gossamer's iridescent flowers. Now gossamer bushes were known by all and kept by none. Even this scant association with birds had been enough to have them removed. The list of taboo objects and activities in Leiodaran culture stretched as long as the memories of those who had lived through the quarantine.

The caller opened her mouth to begin and the shimmer of the robe, the light of the candles, the memories of the tragedy the griot shared, all faded away in the power of her song.

She sang the melody of her creation while the griot droned the lyrics.

As the story went, when birds were outlawed and could no longer be heard at the city's center, a kind of sickness crept up in Leiodarans. Not the sickness that had banished birds to legend and memory but a tangible disquiet, a certain silence between the train's brakes, the rumble of the biplanes, of foot traffic, and the feverish music that had overtaken the sidewalk cafés. People knew what was missing; elements of background noise become more apparent when removed, and even more so when such absence means emptiness—as it did on those silent mornings that skewed the rest of the day. The conundrum of Leiodarans' circumstance weighed on the streets. In the wake of this tide of uneasiness, the callers were created. Now their voices filled the streets in the morning; each of the callers walked their routes, bringing a semblance of peace with their song.

Anna had known bird calls before she came to Leiodare, but they didn't sound like this woman. Some callers had voices that mimicked birds so well that they could trick the mind. This one though, the green-robed woman who walked the path of Anna's street each day, sounded nothing like a bird—not bio, mechanical, or virtual—but Leiodarans didn't seem to care. They revered her. People lined the streets on her route, and Anna had even seen some people throw petals at her feet. This single tangible instance of agreement heartened Anna's impression of her fellow city dwellers. It kept her from believing she'd come to a beautiful, exciting, and function- ally insane place.

What made the woman's song so captivating was not the tenor of her voice, which was pure and pleasing, nor the inflec- tions or absolute control she seemed to have over herself and even Anna's impression of her. It was that the caller seemed to give the best of herself without using words. She commu- nicated as clearly and as profoundly as if she were speaking to Anna from inside her own head. That was why Anna stayed up each night after her shift to listen every morning, and why she stayed now.

The caller's song flowed out over the crowd, ostensibly a background to the story that the griot related, but overpower- ing it easily so that the history took a backseat to the particulars of this moment: the occasional ring of finger cymbals, the smell of burning wax, the heat of the bodies pressed together on the wide avenue.

For a moment Anna closed her eyes, relaxing into the night. It was a brief peace.

Shouts erupted from the crowd, first on the farthest edges north of where Anna stood, but soon closer and more fervent- ly until even the caller quieted her song and turned towards the sound. Just visible in the crush of bodies, Anna could see the shadows of movement in between people's arms and legs as the crowd parted along an invisible axis, creating a path that eventually led straight to her. Anna didn't move. She'd learned in her short time in Leiodare that she rarely feared the same things as the people around her. So she held her ground, squinting through the near darkness as she tried to recognize the wet-looking shadow moving toward her.

Small bodies scurried in the dark. Or rather, on closer inspection, a series of small masses flowed towards her, thousands of rolling beetles falling over each other, surging forward like a glistening wave of tiny legs and hard, clacking bodies. Since the beginning of the rainy season, rolling beetle colonies had infested blocks as far afield as The Shallows, pushing out even the large bee colonies that speckled her neighborhood and the armies of caterpillars in The Dire. From the faint sound of buzzing, Anna suspected that the beetles had lost a fight with one of the nearby colonies and now were pushing humans out of their way.

Just then, a fat raindrop hit Anna square in the middle of her nose, followed by another and another. The hiss of extinguished candles floated across the crowd until it was overtaken by the sound of the rain striking metal, stone, and flesh, a sudden raucous roar. Blinking away the wet, people in the crowd shuffled in all directions, looking for cover. Anna removed her pack and held it low. As she watched the crowd of people start to loosen she quietly unzipped the front pocket and waited. In the instant before the crowd broke apart, Anna held her pack out and scooped off a thin layer of beetles from the rolling wave. Revulsion trickled up her arm. Still, it was surely a week's worth of swan food in one deft swoop. Finally the edges of the crowd started to break away as more people retreated to the spaces between buildings, and towards the train station.

"Please clear the streets!" the unmistakable digital voice of an automated pest sentry urged loudly. Anna turned to the sound and saw the armored sentry rolling slowly onto the street. Within minutes, it would be followed by a full battalion.

"Retire to the comforts of home while the area is cleansed. More concerned citizens please join your brethren at the nearest giene station—." The voice paused and Anna covered her ears. "At 555th and de la Sol."

Anna sighed and looked towards the now-empty platform as she discreetly wiped the straggling beetles from her bag. The caller had fled with the rest of them. Even without the cygnets to consider, she'd rather not endure any time with the "concerned citizens" known to frequent giene stations.

She hoped Peru would answer soon.

3

The sound of metal scraping against stone echoed down McClaren Street. Dr. Eugenio Oliveira passed under the fluffy morning clouds, enjoying the feel of sun on his face. Though he spared a glance or two at the crews working to clear the last of the bright red candle wax from the stoops on the street, his mind and gaze were locked on the next block where the Municipal Rest building stood as stooped and decayed as the residents inside.

Counterbalancing with his attaché case, Eugenio maneuvered to keep his cane from sticking in the gaps between the brick pavers that lined McClaren. As he walked, he dug his cane into the stamps of that founding family's icon printed into the stone. The street had never needed a sign because the pavers were emblematic enough. Later McClaren became infamous for that same founding family's demise when most of them fell victim to the Crumble during the winter of quarantine. As a child, Eugenio had felt sentimentally toward this wide alley of opulence that had once been Leiodare's main thoroughfare; now, as a young man, he only wished it didn't present such a gauntlet.

Eugenio stepped up onto the curb in front of the building and tried to steady himself for the indignity of the moving sidewalk. He grabbed the thick rubber railing just in time to keep his legs from being snatched forward too quickly and sending him into the awkward jerk and tumble with which he'd first greeted the shitspitting thing. Years ago, before the building had been retrofitted for the elderly, chromed banisters had lined the building. The banisters had been just fine with Eugenio, but once the city decided to turn the old tenement into a rest center, the sidewalk went in. Eugenio, despite his knee, shouldn't have to worry about such contraptions for many years to come—but his work required otherwise. Reasonably well balanced, he swatted at a passing bee and spared a glance back down McClaren as Municipal Rest's front doors parted and deposited him inside.

Frigid air conditioning rushed at Eugenio's face as the sidewalk slowly made its way to the front desk junction. A long sparse desk split the lobby into a visitor's waiting area and a resident lounge—there, the administrative manager stood, tapping on the inlaid screen, most likely entering the morning's reports. Ready for the weekly check-in ritual, Eugenio hopped from sidewalk to marble floor.

"Morning, Doctor," the gray-coated man behind the desk said.

"Morning," he responded.

Eugenio pulled up the sleeve of his shirt and scanned his clearance. The day's business downloaded to the tablet in his briefcase while he made small talk with the manager. The tablet beeped completion. Turning for the elevator, Eugenio removed it from his case and prepared for the day's work.

His first interviewee, a short elderly woman with a youthful face and bright white hair, was waiting for him in the hallway when he stepped off the elevator. Interesting that she would get the treatments but let her hair go white, he thought to himself. Eugenio looked forward to getting started.

"Passing your time spying on people, are you?" he asked jokingly.

She harrumphed and stepped into the small apartment.

"They alerted me to your disturbance," she said.

"It's not as if I am an intruder. It's hardly a disturbance for a man to come and visit a new friend," Eugenio replied.

She looked at him sideways, pursing her lips slightly.

"There's no need to humor me with the illusion of friendship. I've had countless confidants in this life and expect to have them in the next. I don't require pity from ambitious young men."

She entered the apartment, leaving the door ajar. Eugenio took this as invitation enough and followed her into the surprisingly sun-washed, cheerful room. He watched her cross the small living room, its walls covered in plaques, and seat herself on the corner of a writing desk along a short wall.

"I apologize for my—" Eugenio began.

"Condescending remarks," she finished for him.

"Yes." Eugenio met her steady gaze. "I meant no disrespect. I apologize."

"Perhaps you were simply overly familiar," she allowed, waving her hand for him to sit. "How can I help you, Dr. Oliveira?"

"Eugenio, please, Dr. Etive. If anyone should be addressed by a title, you are that one." Eugenio reached into his pocket to pull out his pen-sized recorder.

"Now, let's not overcorrect." She made a small noise of exasperation.

Eugenio blinked and looked down at the floor. Absentmindedly, he pulled a small metal circle from his pocket and took a breath as he tried to find a new tack.

"That object, can I see it?" Dr. Etive asked.

He could refuse, of course, but perhaps this would work. He held the charm up at eye level, its concentric circles glinted in the sunlight pouring through the windows.

"Are you Mendejano?" she asked.

Eugenio smiled slightly, impressed by her sharp deductive skills.

"How interesting." Dr. Etive looked at him keenly, seemingly eager now to make his acquaintance. "So, why would a Mendejano become a medical anthropologist?"

"Why not?"

"It's passive. Mendejano fix things, not study them."

"But one must first understand a problem in order to fix it. Don't you agree?" he asked.

"I do. Then you came to be Mendejano later in life?"

"Why do you assume this?" he asked.

"Is it true?" she persisted.

"Somewhat later in life, I am still a young man after all." He chuckled good-naturedly.

"Clearly," she said.

Eugenio stopped laughing. "I'm old enough, Dr. Etive. Old enough to know what the Crumble has done to my home, and yours. We've built not just a society, but a culture on fear." He paused and met her gaze. "We no longer die of the Crumble, but it still steals our lives. Life expectancy in the city has decreased twenty percent since that winter."

"It's just stress," Dr. Etive said in a deadpan voice.

"That's what they say," he answered, "because they have nothing better to say."

Dr. Etive nodded in agreement. He continued.

"I don't know if birds spread the disease, but if they did it's been twenty-five years. Today's medicine far exceeds anything available then. And yet they are still outlawed. It borders on hysteria, and is at least ornithophobic, an entire culture of it. These investigations can lead to the remedy," Eugenio finished.

"The Crumble," she said. "Well-named, how things have deteriorated." She stood and walked toward the kitchen. "Tea?"

Eugenio nodded and watched as Dr. Etive disappeared into the kitchen. He turned up the sensitivity of his recorder.

"So what do you want to know from me?" she asked from the other room.

"I want to know how it started. You were there."

"The whole world knows how it started—Peter Warrel," she answered. The sound of metal on china filled the momentary silence.

Eugenio knew better than most. Researchers from the iCDC concluded that Patient Zero had been Peter Warrel, a visiting engineer from the island of Northern Illinois. He had stayed just long enough to release three infected skin nanos that went on to infect a housekeeping tech as well as the head of the Leiodaran Trust, Eammon McClaren. Shortly thereafter, Peter died in a weeping, curled heap on the bed of his complimentary room in The Spires where he was later found by Frederica Sholt, the unfortunate tech assigned to his corridor.

The two initial carriers, Frederica and Eammon, infected dozens more in the first seventy-two hours of a lackluster conference season and a vigorous carnivale festival. Besides their families, they spread their illness to all Spire guests in the techhouse corridor, the mayor, visiting governor, regional director, the Nepalese ambassador to Chaiwan, and two mistresses. ICDC had even found that Eammon and Frederica had the particular pleasure of re-infecting one another quietly in a corridor, where out of mounting anxiety they touched for the first time, a simple squeeze on a bit of bare shoulder.

"Yes, as well as Sholt and McClaren," Eugenio said.

"A classic case really. Disease usually spreads along the framework of social structure," she responded.

"True, but the iCDC doesn't usually quarantine whole cities—not before or since in fact."

"It was the first superbug. They didn't know any better. Within a week the numbers had exploded into the thousands. On the eighth day they cordoned us off." Dr. Etive walked back into the room, empty-handed. As she spoke, a tray with two slim china carafes floated past her and onto the table between their chairs. "There'd been a carnivale going on, you know. Needless to say with the electrified fences and armed riot brigades, the festivities ended rather abruptly." She settled in the chair opposite Eugenio before she continued.

"For days on end, the broadcasts showed scores of conventioneers and carnivale tourists who had been locked out of their hotel rooms, sleeping in the parks. I saw them myself: the tourists wearing skimpy costumes and smeared face paint. Some of them still had their virtu rigs on. Laughable, but true." She shook her head and gazed into the distance.

Eugenio chuckled softly as he lifted the glass of tea slowly to his lips. Dr. Etive did the same.

"You went out on the streets then?" Eugenio straightened in his seat and moved the recorder closer to Dr. Etive.

"Once. That's all it took to know I didn't want to go back out. Things were much more terrible than they made them seem on the broadcasts: fighting for food and shelter, the horrible little economies that crept up, *rampant* attacks. Of course for all the thousands dying they still spent half their broadcasts talking about a chosen few—celebrities, founding families, a visiting tycoon or two."

"It seems that's when the terror really began—when people realized no one was safe," Eugenio said, thinking of his research. In particular, the speedy and thorough demise of the McClaren family hit Leiodaran news stations in waves, creating a bounty of vid clips and historical lessons on all the family had done to build the city up and how little to protect it from microbes and visiting businessmen. Eugenio would have given anything to interview a McClaren, but virtually the entire family had been wiped out during the quarantine.

"You said you went out once. Why? Where did you go?" Eugenio asked.

"I had to get home," she answered.

"Where had you been?" he asked.

"Out," she answered curtly. "Why did you become a Mendejano later in life? Marriage?"

"No," Eugenio said. He waited for an answer; she did the same.

Eugenio was well-versed in such exchanges—though not in his work. If he exchanged information with every interview subject he would not have come so far in his profession so quickly. Usually Eugenio was a gifted interviewer precisely because he knew what to reveal, but it had been his great pleasure to know a few exceptional people who could draw him out of his premeditated friendliness.

Long before Eugenio joined the research team at Emergency Management he had met magnetic Lucine. She had saved his life and better still saved him from the dread that was his birthright, the same anxieties that plagued other native Leiodarans. When Lucine decided to move to Leiodare he had offered to find a place for them both, not because he wished to share her bed, but very much her time and, at any opportunity, her thoughts, relentless and deep as the ocean. So he had found a small compound beyond The Shallows, nestled between two empty warehouses. They'd decorated it with the concentric circles of the Mendejano, blessed it in a ceremony that made them brother and sister, ate of each other's flesh and became soul twins. What they had was better than marriage and he would betray her to no one. He knew what Dr. Etive was fishing for, but she'd come back empty on this particular line of questioning.

Dr. Etive sipped her tea and placed the carafe back down on the tray.

"'A soul without a bird to carry it beyond is doomed to forever walk the streets of its regrets.' Isn't that a central Mendejano belief? This city then would seem the last place to be," she said.

"Or the first," Eugenio replied.

"You *are* an ambitious young man." She paused. "It can be a dangerous trait, you know."

"As is fear. . . I became a Mendejano because of a brush with mortality," Eugenio answered.

Dr. Etive finished her tea and brought the cup gently down onto the tray.

"On the day the Crumble began, my husband and I had been out at an affair that our friend Rory hosted regularly, on the other side of town," Dr. Etive offered. She raised an eyebrow at Eugenio, waiting. "I don't know why I didn't contract the disease, but I didn't."

"And this Rory, that you and your husband were visiting, is he available for an interview?" Eugenio asked.

"You mean, is he dead?" she replied. "He's a ghost now."

"Excuse me?" Eugenio asked.

"I said, he's a ghost. It's Rory McClaren. So you tell me."

4

Even after seventy-three years of good health, Rory McClaren still stockpiled medicine, hoarded food, and did not ever, under any circumstances, share his quarters with anyone. Though he knew his family had not necessarily died out those many years ago because of their proximity to each other, he took the precaution of living his life utterly alone, at the tip of The Spires where he could look down upon the city, but never touch it.

He stood now at one of the floor-to-ceiling windows that encased his penthouse, with one eye pushed into his monstrously expensive telescope. He watched a chattering of Starlings loitering near The Spires. The teenagers had their hands shoved into their pockets as they cajoled their way through the early evening. The customary dusters that all Starlings wore swirled above the sidewalk as they moved, putting on more of show than the people that wore them. This particular group was less than interesting, not like yesterday's mob of girls tearing up and down Tindle Avenue, or last week's colorful display of territorial behavior in The Dire. Rory checked the time and abandoned the scene at the window. He was late for a city government dinner.

"Closed circuit Monitor I-7," he said, commanding the immense screen in the great room to life. Instantly the banquet hall of the Arts Guild materialized. A lone morning caller, a handsome Asian man dressed in blue, stood at the head of a long banquet table filled with dark-suited officials and their companions. Each of the other morning callers, resplendent in their respective signature color, was evenly spaced around the table. The caller in blue began to sing, filling Rory's penthouse with the sound of morning.

Because Rory enjoyed space more than spectacle, his rooms were sparsely decorated. The library consisted of a collection of old discs, a long mahogany table and one of the first virtu booths that used to dot the city back before the outbreak. The great room held two long divans, a holo projector, wall screen, and his virtu setup, including a top-of-the-line viewer and pack, available only to him as the sole heir of the McClaren family. His walls were windows, spectacular sheets of crystal clear plexi that could withstand hurricane-force winds. He'd chosen thick carpeting for the great room, so thick that he left footsteps behind making it seem sometimes as if he were surrounded by invisible men. The kitchen floor was smoothed rock, and in his bedroom self-sustaining grass never grew, but always comforted, reminding Rory of the world before.

By any measure his penthouse was superior to the apartment in which he'd endured the winter of the Crumble, worrying about his family and peering out of the basement windows to discern what was left of the city. He'd spent the entire season locked away in the small apartment he usually reserved for his more hair-raising dalliances. That Afternoon—he still referred to it that way when Rory spoke of it to himself—he'd been holed up with a free-minded couple, pushing the bounds of endurance and invention when the news reports began.

The reports rolled in and soon dominated every channel and subscription service, the number of dead steadily rising. Rory had extricated himself from the complicated embrace and, sweat still on his brow, stared at the holo report projecting in the middle of the room with mounting uneasiness. He'd called over to the family place and received no response, even on the dedicated line. The robe his nieces had bought him for his birthday lay on the divan near the bed; he grabbed it and stood, fully intending to collect his faculties and devise a course of action. Instead he found himself staring at the newscast. Soon after he shooed the couple away, locked the door behind them and did not leave that place for the entire three months of the quarantine.

Even now in the great room of the penthouse, a room that could have held the entire Leoiodaran Dance Theater, a full coterie of brass players, violinists and hover artists, the thought of people joining him made his scalp itch. He watched the performance on the giant screen in front of him and tried to ignore the faint tingling above his left ear. True enough, the strong young caller performing had a certain quality beyond his handsomeness, but even his obvious distractions wouldn't be enough to keep Rory's mind off of escape and so he sat in the delicious emptiness of his penthouse, watching the performance via the closed-circuit feed that the city provided to Rory for all official functions. As the only surviving McClaren it behooved the city government to find a way to use his cache and perhaps woo him into remembering the city when the time came to settle his final affairs. Rory really couldn't blame them—even now the McClaren fortune was vast, and Leiodare, like an insecure lover, required tremendous upkeep lest it buckle under the pressure of its own delusions.

The McClarens originally earned their fortune with The Last Word. Until then no one had applied hologram projection technology to the funereal market, and as Rory's grandfather, Pop Pop, loved to say on the many occasions that he recounted how they had come to be *those* McClarens, "People will spend their last dime to get the last word." And so that's what his grandfather named the technology, focus group results be damned. In actuality, the levity of the name boosted the brand appeal. It softened the shock of those first few families who sat quietly at wakes until they were suddenly faced with their departed loved one standing at the front of the room, perfectly attired and themselves to the last detail—in some instances standing next to their own coffins, seeming just as solid and certainly bearing a greater resemblance than what was left in the box. Pop Pop also loved to share how some family members fainted at the "miraculous sight."

His favorite story involved the famous Finnish soccer player who had had a heart attack when he heard his beloved mother's voice just as clear as it had been when she last saw him—no audio hiss, no pops, clicks or startup chimes. "Virtually indistinguishable," Pop Pop would say. And while known to crack jokes at everyone's expense, Pop Pop had better judgment in business. He found the best and brightest holo techs available and when it became necessary, supplemented their craftsmanship with the innovation of leading neuro researchers and surgeons. These brilliant men and women surpassed his own financial projections when they created a new technology that made The Last Word look like a parlor trick.

So while The Last Word became the gold standard for funerals, the tech it had spawned, virtu, nearly took over the world. It had multifaceted allure: users could experience events they never would have in their own lives, and not just a hallucination or an approximation, but an experience that felt like any other. Virtu linked straight into the brain; it used the same neural centers as one's eyes, skin, ears, and all. This coupled with a revolutionary nano interface shut all other competitors out of the market for a decade. A virtu user could truly experience the world through someone else's eyes; that application alone revolutionized anthropology, profiling, even legislation, and a steady black market of crime reals surfaced trading in snuff to sex, and things much darker.

People got hooked and rarely put virtu back down once they picked it up. Analysts insisted that the wave would crest, but it kept coming steady and unmistakable as the tide. Restrictions were enacted; laws passed, and flouted. But by then, virtu in greater and lesser degrees was everywhere. Leiodare remained its epicenter. McClaren Industries' research and development, administrative, and operations centers were headquartered in the city before the Crumble.

Rory had first tried virtu at five years old. At the family's annual Thanksgiving celebration, his Pop Pop stood, rotund and regal, in the middle of the room, wine glass in hand and a prototype viewer and pack on the table next to him. In the middle of a loud recitation of how he'd watched the first Spire built from an office he had leased across the street specifically for that purpose, Pop Pop cut himself off, and beckoned to young Rory who had just walked into the room.

"But that was the past. And here is the future. Rory my boy, come to your Pop Pop. I've something to show you."

Rory excitedly stepped forward, expecting a treat from one of Pop Pop's travels, a seashell from upper Mongolia or perhaps a surgechip from the outlying colonies—but instead his grandfather set a pair of very heavy, opaque shades over his eyes.

"To block out the room," his Pop Pop explained to the group of assembled family.

Rory heard his mother's voice, saying, "Dad. What is this now?"

"This is Rory's fortune. All of our fortunes. Don't worry. He's about to get the first taste of what will be the humanity's next must-have."

"Dad—" she said.

Rory heard a click, and his life was replaced by another. The warm room of aunts and uncles was gone. He saw a lush canopy of treetops and above him an expanse of sky stretched out from one end of the world to the other. Strong sun beat down on him. His back felt almost too hot. The sweet potent scent of expensive flowers replaced the smell of roast pheasant. He looked down at a large brown hand that rested in what felt like his lap. A breeze caressed his face.

Everything went black.

"I don't think that's a good idea," his mother said as she lifted the glasses from Rory's head. He blinked, utterly dazed, and looked around at his family, expecting them to stir in a breeze.

"You think I'd put it on him if it weren't safe? He's fine," Pop Pop said.

"You don't know that, Dad."

His mother had been right. Rory had not been fine, not since then. He'd been rough and tumble and pushing himself beyond boundaries. His time in the trees had become hardwired into his personality and from then on Rory sought thrills. He wanted to repeat that first sensation of adventure and freedom that he'd found up in the treetops of someone else's mind.

He kayaked around Leiodare, did late-night base drops from The Spires, joined the service for missions into the Deserts, and until that winter of isolation in his forty-eighth year he lived each moment as if it were being recorded. In his early twenties, he'd even created a few virtu reals of his own and floated them onto the market anonymously, compensated enough by the thought of others experiencing his exploits. In each real, he tried to rival the moment in the canopy that had come to define living for him. But by then virtu didn't satisfy him. After that single week of recording for others, virtu became an occasional sex toy and not much more.

Rory rediscovered virtu alone in the apartment during those anxious winter months after the outbreak. When his solitude became permanent, virtu life replaced the one he had locked away from himself.

No doubt he made a good ghost story, he thought as he watched the city officials on the closed circuit feed. Creepy old man McClaren. Gone were the people who remembered Rory of Yore: the thick black hair and warm amber eyes, the broad shoulders, his way with women, and with men. Rory of Yore: once the title had been an easy seduction strategy—a complement to the well-honed physique, the family name and its attendant air of wealth. Now it seemed a cruel but effective irony—good only for an edgy chuckle between glasses of syrah and meditation. During the winter of the Crumble, Rory of Yore had fallen down a hole, one created in his boyhood, but carefully covered over with conquest since then. In the decades of isolation it had opened and grown so that to Rory it seemed that he lived at the bottom of the world, and not in a tower whose height rivaled that of the mountains surrounding Leiodare.

Virtu put him back where he belonged. As the single largest stockholder of McClaren Industries he had not only the prototypes for the first models, but received the latest updates to the technology, and he used his special benefits in earnest: the feather-light streaming gear, as well as a full-body submersion unit that allowed him to block out the world completely and hook himself up to extrasensory points. The tank—as he referred to the large clear box in the corner of his living room—delivered a life crisper, clearer and more exciting than actual life had ever been—even living out on the edges of experience as Rory often had. There were no worries in virtu, no hesitations, no doubts or recriminations, no disappointments. You knew at the end of your tryst in a Tuscan vineyard, or the climb up Mount Kilimanjaro, that the glasses came off and you would return safely to your life without any consequences for the actions you'd just experienced—not for you or your loved ones. Life could not compete with that.

It had never been able to. From the first booth-sized confessionals that once dotted the city, to the prototype of a cranial implant scheduled to hit the market next quarter and now glowing orange inside a small plexi case near Rory's kitchen, virtu beckoned and seduced with its artificial perfection.

Rory turned up the sound on the closed circuit feed. Too much of the caller's song was lost on his failing hearing aids.

He hadn't gone cricket deaf, but as most of his hearing was linked straight into his brain from the virtus he didn't much use his ears and so did not miss the sensation except at times like these. With the exception of his sight, he'd let all his external senses fade when his wealth could easily have saved, even enhanced, his perception. He'd kept his sight sharp so he could spy from The Spires, his only direct connection to the rest of the world.

The caller's song reverberated through the great room bouncing off of the triple-paned plexi. Rory knew even if someone had been standing on the other side of the glass or on the never-used balcony they wouldn't be able to hear the song. The Spires' insulation was part of its beauty. Even as a boy he had found the buildings breathtaking, a shard of a fairy tale sunk deep in the jungle soil. After his true home, the family home, had been lost to him because of his own fear, he'd come here because of that boy's musings. Even now, Rory sometimes wondered if he didn't live inside the last remnant of the Leiodaran dream.

Rory closed his eyes and listened. The caller's song, as lovely as it was, reinforced the demise of that idea of Leiodare. The song was a refined imitation, but an imitation nonetheless. Rory hadn't truly enjoyed a song since Peru's last virtu real had been delivered, many months before.

The memory opened a blankness in him; he let the song fill it, for the moment.

5

Crisp night air blew into Anna's face as she made her way down the avenue towards Acte Station. As she approached the stairs that led down into the station, she switched her shopping bag of parcels from hand to hand, plucked her sunglasses from her inner pocket and put them on. For the few seconds she walked in the dark, she tilted the frames down and looked over the straight rim.

Bright light bled up from the underground station, creating a block of light on the sidewalk. When she reached the top stair, Anna squinted and put the glasses back in their proper place.

Giene light filled the station. A whiter version of the cheap yellow giene light in Anna's loft flooded every crevice of the station, bouncing against the white tile and red trim. Another level below, at the tracks and benches some transportation engineer had had the presence of mind to build colored gel boxes around the most powerful recessed giene lights, creating both red and gold spotlights that shone down in focused beams. Experience had taught Anna that a group of five or so people could fit in the beam, and standing in it could blast the chill from her bones on a cold day, help clear her mind on a cloudy one. She suspected the result to be more serendipity than design. Standing there she always felt as if was next to be called on stage or perhaps handpicked for whatever daydream of redemption overtook her that day. Now standing in a wide golden beam, Anna placed her bag between her feet. The mouth of the shopping bag opened wider and Anna stared down at the parcels inside: a package of figs and a pair of handkerchiefs for her latest package to Peru.

A soft hum bounced around the station and Anna looked up at an almond-skinned woman with nearly shoulder-length dreadlocks at the far end of the station. Even from this distance, Anna could tell she was attractive. Her features weren't clear, but nicely proportioned and somehow familiar, fitting in the pattern of beauty. She wore a bright white pantsuit with no jacket or shirt, just a fitted vest that showed off her shapely arms and décolletage. The pants fit in the right places as well.

The woman stood in a beam of red light swaying slightly as she hummed.

Anna tried to nonchalantly focus in on the sound without turning towards her. The melody seemed familiar if not the words. A small group of people—a middle-aged male couple and their female friend laughed and talked on the platform between Anna and the woman. Anna slowly moved towards the woman and away from the noise, the beginnings of recognition tugging at her.

"Borrowed Love," was it? Perhaps one of the torch songs from the 88s? A bramble of likely candidates clustered in Anna's mind, each one batted away with the next note she heard in the mesmerizing melody echoing through the train station.

As Anna leaned against the supporting pillar a few meters away from the woman, the song resolved itself as Anna hummed along quietly. "The Life of Ever."

Of course. How could Anna have not known it from the first verse?

She'd listened to the song so much during her travels that the audio track had become inoperable, but even then she still heard the refrains in her sleep and first thing in the morning. It was a comfort she didn't know she needed at the time. She smiled to herself and sang a bit more freely than she realized.

She felt a tingling at her shoulder and inched her gaze up. The woman was watching her, eyes squinting as she tried to discern mocking or perhaps trying to place Anna's face. Looking at her confirmed the familiarity, the pattern Anna had recognized. She knew the woman humming "The Life of Ever"—the voice, even at a hum, was as unmistakable as her lips.

It was her caller, the green-robed morning that Anna stayed up until all hours of the night to catch. Uncovered, the caller rivaled the beauty of her songs—in much the same way. It was unexpected, but perfectly in proportion—plump lips, almond brown eyes, strong jaw, and the hint of dimples in her heart-shaped face. Her voice, of course, had been the same, just more subdued, and warmer when wrapped around words. Also something else Anna couldn't place until she realized they were still staring at each other. Her voice was more personal.

Wind rushed ahead of the oncoming train. Anna looked towards it and felt her caller watching her. She kept her eyes on the train as it slowed, and stopped. When she looked back the caller was gone, already onboard. Anna entered the next car. She looked for a place to sit, perhaps behind a pillar, but one with the vantage point of the window separating cars. As the car shifted its weight around a semi-circle in the track, Anna let go to the momentum and slid to the back of the seat. She caught a glimpse of the caller, eyes closed, still humming she bet, filling the space up with her song.

The train approached McClaren Street, Anna's stop. She sat and watched as the doors opened and closed. She'd been intermittently examining the contents of her shopping bags and slyly (she hoped) stealing looks at the caller in the next car. Now Anna stared openly. How many mornings had she spent, making cups of tea waiting for the woman's voice to pierce the fading night? She'd scuffed an impression of her backside on the windowsill from sitting where she watched the caller, with her feet up on the railing of the fire escape, her back to the loft and open window. Invariably at some point in her song, Anna closed her eyes and it felt like floating.

Anna had once stayed at the Etoran beaches for a virtuoso assignment where the client only required that she float for hours in salt-rich waters and stare at the sun. They had been some of the best days of her life. The water covered her ears, blocking nearly all sound. Strange then that the sound of this woman's voice would call up the memory of bobbing freely, safely with only the sky and a warm, soft sun hiding behind clouds for company—but still in that isolation feeling connected to each and every thing.

And now that same voice—articulated in a striking heart-shape-faced beauty—sat just a few meters away, exposed and accessible as anyone else in the city. Even the cygnets could wait for that.

The train sped up as it descended into The Shallows. When the caller got out two stops later, Anna followed.

Nightlife ruled The Shallows. A few places offered family-friendly distractions during the day, but they were far outnumbered by other attractions. After dark, the clubs threw open their doors to entice Leiodarans to come and work off their various tensions. Passing by the station lockers, Anna considered depositing the parcels inside, but didn't want to lose sight of the caller, so she walked briskly on. The caller could duck in one of a score of entrances and be lost to Anna forever until she reappeared some morning shrouded and distant as ever. Anna couldn't take the chance and so instead stuck relatively close to the caller. Anna ascended the stairs no more than a few meters behind the well-shaped back and the white fabric that accentuated it. As she came up the stairs and back into darkness, Anna abandoned her sunglasses. Up above, the omnipresence of bright water briefly made her reconsider.

Tenea D. Johnson

Long before the land that became Leiodare had been reborn as a jungle, before the dry city that had preceded Leiodare, before cities, an asteroid had struck this stretch of earth and left behind its impression. The resultant impact crater stretched six kilometers in every direction. Apparently some long-ago city planner had thought it intriguing to not only build inside it, but to fill the crater with water and construct an elevated thoroughfare from which one could look down on the resultant canal that ran around the edges of the buildings. Dozens of light globes floated on the water year round. Some of the first residents had introduced the light globes, in homage to the Chaiwanese immigrants that had come to inhabit The Shallows long ago. Now The Shallows was awash in glowing orbs, large and small. They dotted the moving water and mirrored the constant movement of bodies on the streets.

The entrances of buildings in The Shallows were at thoroughfare level; some on stilts, others huddled up together on wooden pylons. On the small service lanes that branched out from the main thoroughfare, the water was held back by a clear waterproof barrier, and there buskers and independent dance troupes vied for attention.

Up on the main thoroughfare, cavernous dance halls competed with small, exclusive clubs of every hue and distinction—sex clubs, dance clubs, clubs that were essentially enormous kitchens where guests could prepare or devour every delicacy known. Everywhere sound abounded—music, live and recorded, laughter, shrieks and a steady hum of conversation below the rest. Anna knew that she should get back on the train and go home. She hadn't checked on the cygnets since this morning. And, she must look a fool carrying her parcels through The Shallows on a party night. Besides, following people—even beautiful intriguing women with whom she'd shared every morning for the last year—was not a usual or welcome action on her part.

The caller crossed the street and, a block later, so did Anna.

She was getting closer to the other woman, walking a few paces to the caller's left, an old habit of hers to let people see her when she followed near them on the street. It was a way of letting them know they had nothing to fear from her. She did it now, thinking that the other woman probably wouldn't recognize her from the train. Anna doubted that she was memorable enough to be careful and she didn't want to be careful, didn't want to think there was a devious reason behind her walk through The Shallows.

Perhaps the isolation had finally gotten to her—and this was the beginning of some new and shameful chapter of her life. Trouble was, she didn't quite believe it, even as she continued to match her footsteps to the caller's, continued to watch her lithe back as she moved down the street. Anna caught a glimpse of herself in a looking glass on the corner and tried to pat her thick, dark hair into place—didn't ask herself why.

The caller slowed down in front of a nondescript gray building in the midst of the glare and pomp of the others on the block. Anna slowed her pace as well.

The caller stopped near the entrance, a gold-colored door, and looked back Anna's way, her eyebrows knitted together.

"Are you lost?" she asked, an edge of challenge in her tone.

Her speaking voice was raspy with a slight mellow accent Anna couldn't place. Anna watched the movement of her lips and worked to clear her head enough to answer. She felt embarrassed, but oddly forthright.

"No," she flicked across the other woman's gaze. "Not lost."

The caller's shoulders moved down; her eyebrows relaxed and the creases in her forehead disappeared. "Not lost. But searching."

"Know of any good places to go around here?" Anna asked. She cringed on the inside.

"Depends on what you're looking for."

"Good music. There's something, a song, but I can't remember the name."

A man approached the caller from behind, a ready smile on his face.

"Seife, how you are, sweet?" he asked, moving in for a brief hug.

"I am well." Seife turned to at Anna, raised her eyebrows in invitation, looking from the door to Anna and back. She followed the man into the club.

Anna smiled and stepped inside, savoring the ring of this new sound: Seife.

Fine particles of gold glitter swirled around the dimly lit club, settling in drinks, on shoulders, and on the small stage Seife walked towards. Anna took a seat at the bar and ordered.

All manner of Leiodarans filled the small, circular tables crowded around the stage: men in business attire with precious onyx pieces at the collar and cuff, students in their finest, artists and bedraggled office workers who hadn't bothered to change on the way, folks who from their server aprons seemed to be on break from other spots on the street. They shared their rapture and their release watching as Seife and her piano accompanist, the man from outside, began to weave jazz and percussobeat into a rich tapestry unfurled for their pleasure.

As the bartender deposited a tall glass in front of Anna, she turned to find Seife now standing in front of a baby grand while her accompanist played a slow-building tale of betrayal and redemption on the banks of a distant shore as imagined by the songwriter and rendered by Seife's voice.

Anna leaned against the bar, swirling the brown around the edges of her drink until it melded with the blue liqueur that would make it easy to sleep tonight. She usually didn't indulge in somatics, but tonight she needn't stay up for the dawn. Her call had come early. It was not quite a call though. This was more than the visceral sounds of morning that the callers created. Tonight was a night of words, an articulating night: "Seife," lyrics, whatever it was Anna intended to say later which right now she wasn't quite sure of.

A talking night, perhaps a night of connections, however brief. Anna had once been to a club down the avenue, and had met a counselor from Nashville. They'd spent two nights together and then none as Anna pulled away when it came time to prepare a package for Peru's birthday. Anna thought the counselor had moved back to Nashville or maybe somewhere further over the mountains.

"This seat occupied?" A young woman, stylish and fresh, even in her office attire, stood in front of Anna, blocking her view. The music and glitter swirled around the woman so that she almost seemed to stand in a fog. Anna looked down at the seat next to her.

"Yes. I'm afraid it is," Anna replied, looking briefly at the woman's face and then around her to focus on the stage again. She didn't see the woman walk away so much as feel relief when once again her view was unobstructed.

The lyrics slipped past Anna's ears so that they almost seemed to mean nothing. She'd been sure the song was about fucking and foreign exchanges, but now it seemed to be more a love story. She looked down at her glass and wondered what role the somatics played in her confusion. The other glasses in the room were filled with orange and green liquids. She seemed to be the only one imbibing in somatics. But the other patrons looked as dreamy as she felt, maybe from the music or perhaps the company they kept; she seemed to be the only person here alone. The young office worker she had rebuffed had already found another seat to occupy.

The caller finished her set and, to Anna's excitement and uneasiness, walked her way. As Seife moved, the deep V of the white vest contrasted with her skin, further emphasizing her cleavage, the slightly muscled arms, the collarbone and graceful neck. Though Anna stared, she didn't feel self-conscious. She worked at keeping her expression as neutral as possible, but doubted that she succeeded. When Anna saw the caller's bemused smile, she was certain she'd failed. For a moment she tensed, expecting the worst. She tried to think of something clever to say and said something else entirely as Seife gracefully sat on the stool next to her own.

"Beautiful," Anna said.

Seife watched her a few seconds before answering, whether sizing her up or gathering her patience, Anna couldn't be sure.

"Different from what I sing in the mornings, though," Seife said.

"I thought you weren't supposed to tell people who you were."

"True. It's a special secret only shared with rich donors and politicians. Makes them feel important. Or maybe to feed the delusion." Seife looked at her silently again—this time definitely sizing her up.

"Well, don't I feel important then," Anna said.

"You should. But not because of that."

Anna felt the heat rising to her face, and was momentarily taken aback by the sensation. In a sort of stupor, she continued. "And why is that? According to you?"

Seife seemed pleased with the hint of edge in Anna's reply.

"You have no reason to feel important?"

"I never said that. I just wanted to hear your supposition. You are the caller after all." She'd lowered her voice without thinking about it on the last sentence.

"'After all'. I don't think I have ever heard someone use that phrase before. 'After all'; how it that possible really? To know something after all? Are you not part of the all?"

Anna was both surprised and excited by this line of questioning. Parts of her reserved for quiet reading and heated arguments with the media broadcasts began to stir and take note of Seife with mounting interest.

"It is a paradox. After all, I wouldn't even be Anna anymore. Much less would you hold the same job."

"Anna?" Seife asked.

"Anna Armour."

"Armour, a French surname?" Seife asked.

"My surname is mongrel. Armour is part of my first name. It's Anna Armour."

"You said. . ." Seife began.

"I don't usually tell people the whole thing."

"A night of secrets revealed."

"Yes," Anna agreed. Silence settled between them while this sank in.

"It is not a job, they say. Callers are called," Seife said.

"I didn't mean to—" Anna began.

"I know," Seife interrupted. "Why don't you usually tell people your whole name?"

"They're usually just asking to be polite. No need to know more than is necessary. . . Or perhaps I'm just lazy," Anna said.

"So you're feeling energetic then? Or you're feeling impolite?"

Anna left that one unanswered, turned the bar stool to face Seife more fully. "Why do you have to cover your face when you call? Why do you agree to it?"

"You are quite forthright."

Anna looked down at the bar, swirling the dark liquid in her glass. "I am tonight."

"You believe that this is the drink," Seife suggested.

Anna lifted her gaze back up from the bar and shook her head slightly. "No, not the drink."

Seife smiled softly, and turned slowly on her stool, back towards the stage.

"Time for my next set. Perhaps I'll tell you later," Seife said. She acknowledged Anna with a nod of her head.

"Anna." Seife stepped off the stool and looked back at Anna, her eyes inching from shoes all the way up until their gazes briefly met, then she turned away.

Anna watched the shapely back recede from her. Glitter dust swirled in the air Seife's body displaced as she moved, the sparkling fragments spiraling in her wake.

Eyelids heavy, and with the warmth of the liquor languor deep in Anna's bones, she could almost sleep where she sat. She concentrated on not resting her head on her crossed arms, though they felt as drawn together as two magnets. She let the thought float away as Seife began to sing. The familiar lyrics reached Anna though her haze.

Ever was born on the brink
Of two moments
crashing together in time
She flew before walking
Sang before talking
And traded her soul for a dime.

It had been her mother's favorite song. Seife's version had jazz where the original was folk, making it less a tragedy, but listening to it, Anna's excitement began to dissipate, her mood to dim. The somatics didn't help. She felt at any moment she might cry, or pass out, or otherwise embarrass herself. The caller had been kind, even interested in bantering with her, but she'd perhaps been foolish to think it were anything more. Perhaps. Anna leaned over to the bartender, nearly upending her drink, and asked when Seife would next perform. She heard herself slur, but couldn't find the edges of her words so they all tumbled out together. She turned back to the stage and slowly her vision followed. She didn't have long before she'd be unable to get herself home. With a last, lingering look at Seife, she stepped back out the club's golden door.

❖ ❖ ❖

On the train, Anna leaned her head back with eyes closed. She tried to pull herself out of her mood with planning: she should look in on the cygnets as soon as she got home, check for new reals in The Dire—her mother would have hated that place almost as much as she would have enjoyed tonight's performance. Anna's to-do list drifted away at the thought. It was no use trying not to think of her mother. She let her mind wander.

Until Peru, Anna had only been close to one other person. Her mother, Bly, was pressed so deeply into Anna's soul that her emotions ran around the edges of Bly until they emptied out Anna's pen, her paint, her charcoal—all of it touching her mother before it touched paper. Bly had impressed everyone. It was the reason behind her mother's string of successes, and ultimately Anna believed the reason she'd found herself wandering through the woods at fourteen, let loose on the world without her mother's guidance.

Most mothers encouraged their little girls to attend dance class, or learn a third language, or spend time in zero-G workshops. Not Bly. Anna didn't attend classes with other children. Instead, her mother bought Anna her first set of paints when most parents would have been horrified at the thought. It had quieted the intense headaches that plagued Anna.

Anna most appreciated it, though, because art gave her friends to play with, if only those made of paper and clay. Bly knew art would help the headaches because she'd been through the same ordeal, but her parents had not known what to do, for Bly or with her.

Bly only taught Anna the old art styles: no nanos or holo pens; they wouldn't have fit the need. And as Bly told her, there'd be time enough for nanos.

Anna would sit with Bly in their lab—she had always insisted on calling it this as far back as Anna could remember—and marvel at the splotches of green and purple that Anna made on the roll of banner paper spread out on the floor. They spent hours together there. So much so that until she learned to write properly, Anna thought her name was three green stars. The image felt so right, that if she were a thing she believed then these are the things she would be.

Bly let Anna paint the bottom meter of her bedroom wall and a kitchen chair that found its way into the back of the lab. With each project—large or small, planned or accidental—Bly intently watched Anna while she drew. When Anna turned three years old, her mother began to explain the importance of Anna's work.

"It's a safe way to create, to practice," her mother said to her from where they both sat at their worktables, Bly's a bigger version of her own.

"Safe," Anna repeated happily. She looked up at her mother, smiling.

Bly laughed. Anna watched as she grabbed a small bottle of red juice from the corner of her large worktable.

"Something new today, Anna," her mother said, climbing down from her chair and kneeling near Anna. "Let's start a new one, love." Her mother placed a fresh sheet of paper on her desk and filled an empty container with a bit of the red juice. To this, her mother added some of the blue paint she'd been using to draw clouds. Mixed together, the juice and paint created a rich purple liquid that immediately caught her attention.

"This juice has bugs in it," her mother said. Anna looked at her wide-eyed and squinted at the bottle of juice. She couldn't see any bugs, but her mother never, ever lied; so she waited for further explanation.

"The bugs are what made the juice red," Bly continued.

Anna blinked, taking it in.

"Bugs like this," Bly said removing her handheld from her back pocket and showing Anna an image of a small red beetle.

"You're gonna bring the bugs back."

Anna looked at her mother incredulously.

Bly laughed out loud, shaking her head. "You can do it, love. Draw Mommy a picture of this bug. Just look at it, feel it in here," she said, placing one hand on Anna's chest and another on her head, "and draw it." Her mother placed her hands in her lap and smiled, waiting.

Anna took her paintbrush and dipped it into the purple liquid. Without hesitation she drew what looked like a purple oval of sun with six short rays, or at best a squashed bug. She placed the brush back on its pad and looked over at her mother.

"Good job, Anna," her mother said.

Within a minute the image began to vibrate on the paper. Anna moved closer to the paper and stared. Awkwardly the bug lurched up and forward, trying its best to climb out of the paper.

"That's my girl." Her mother scooped the strange insect into her palm, then deposited it into a small aquarium she pulled out from behind a stack of paints and wax on the floor.

Anna looked at the thing through the glass and smiled proudly.

"What should we call her, Anna?" her mother asked.

Ms. Janks, as the bug came to be known, lived just long enough to witness the birth of her successor, inadvertently teaching Anna about the ultimate consequence of creation: death.

Anna took the death of Ms. Janks in stride, though the responsibilities of living, even then, caused her moments of pause. Bly taught her that she must never create for personal gain, that it was best to sit with the work before she began so that she could absorb its essence from the genetic material, and most importantly, she should maintain her humility. Anna, like all children, hadn't understood the logic behind placing limits on herself. So, in the beginning, she often had to stop and consider her impulse, if only after she had followed it.

Anna's training and art progressed; her acumen for each appeared boundless. Her painting became more vibrant and life-like with a depth of texture and tone that began to rival the pieces that she and Bly saw on their frequent trips to museums. Bly supplemented Anna's work with lessons on organic chemistry and biology so that over time, her drawings slowly became more realistic, and in turn so did her creations. She painted and drew nearly every day, but Bly only had her create things slowly, every few months and sometimes not for a year at a time.

"You're not ready for that yet" became a refrain of Anna's prepubescent years. She started printmaking and sculpture—but her non-artistic creation lagged behind. Anna could tell, though, with what Bly did let her do and the improving results that her mother was pleased with her progress. Soon they would try a joint project, Bly declared while she examined a small cherry tree Anna had made with a woodcut block. No more than a half-meter tall, the tree was exquisite, its branches winnowy and windblown, the blossoms perfectly formed puffs of blush. Bly barely touched them as she peered at the tiny tree from all sides.

"It's beautiful, Anna," her mother had said. "You're ready. We'll start our project in the summer."

"What project?" Anna had asked.

Bly turned from the tree and spoke directly to her.

"Do you know how many plant and animals species have become extinct just in the last five years? More than six times the rate of a century ago. Some of those could survive if a single food source in their habitats were reestablished, or they were brought back in a different location. If enough of them are made, they'll survive. That wouldn't be a new fantasy, Anna, but a new world, with the right old and the best of the new. Together we could start that."

For Bly, that summer never came, and never did her world. And so for Anna there had been no one until Peru.

Anna opened her eyes. She must have been in a fugue; the twenty-minute ride home was nearly over.

Groggily, Anna lifted her head and squinted as the train slowed at McClaren Station. As she stepped into the bright burgundy beam where she'd first seen Seife, she realized that she'd left the parcels for Peru back at the club.

6

Eugenio woke before his alarm. He reached up to the touch-pad next to the bed and pulsed the wall sconces fully on. Before he could turn onto his back, he heard his sister, Lucine, open the door.

"You're going to be late," Lucine said from the doorway. He looked up and saw her standing with a ripe glistenberry in one hand. She chomped down on on it as she crossed the room and stood over him. "They're gonna fire you if you keep showing up late and then what?"

He could hear the smile in her voice.

"A bit early for gloating, no? Besides, I'm early." He turned over on his back just as a drop of the berry's juice fell from her palm and down onto his cheek.

"Never too early." She smiled down at him. "I'm just saying this is no way to get there first if indeed you intend to. Breakfast?" Her long, dark hair brushed his nose from where she stood. Lucine always wore it down in the morning, a thick black drape that fell past her waist and made her almost unbelievably lovely: the midnight hair, the smooth olive skin, sparkling brown eyes and chiseled measured jaw. Though he loved the intimacy of these moments, Eugenio wasn't quite comfortable with the feeling that crept up with them.

Lucine produced another fruit from the pocket of her jacket.

He reached up to take it, then watched as she left his room. Eugenio finished the fruit and got dressed for work. Stepping outside his bedroom into the huge open space of their industrial loft, he didn't see Lucine—not in the bare concrete of the kitchen or in her workshop near the service elevator. He walked toward the elevator and spied Lucine through the glass door that led out onto the mezzanine roof. Lucine sat on the ledge. He knew she could spend hours staring out in the haze of the city in the predawn dew. She liked to start her mornings this way, with only the quiet hum of the building and the faint lights of the wakening city at her back, The Dumps in front of her.

She had told him that the great mounds of indeterminate black and brown, the chunks of varying depth beckoned to her and something would always catch her attention: the oddly shaped something in the distance, a glare near the middle, something to be investigated, the latest possibility lying out there on the mound.

Eugenio opened the glass door that led out to the roof.

". . . is the future. My knowledge is old, passed to me from mouth to mind," Lucine said. She paused for a moment and with her back to him raised her hand so it was a bit further from her mouth. Eugenio saw the small recorder there, an old one he'd given her months ago. She had always been much better at this part of being Mendejano than him. She had gigs of oral histories backed up and broadcast, but as much as he liked to record other people's stories, he didn't yet have any of his own. He listened as she continued.

"I am a toolmaker, still rare for a woman. Tools themselves are still necessary even in this virtual world. People do not know this until they need one. And that is when I appear."

She was a great storyteller, Eugenio thought, and almost as if she had heard the thought she said:

"Once upon a time, healing took only a few breaths. This is how my ancestors did it: a mouthful of smoke blown over the right face with the right words at the right time. And of course the right smoke. Now those herbs are harder to come by as the pharmas took what they wanted and the world poisoned the rest. So we have evolved. I don't share my ancestors' religion, but we do have the same beliefs. We Mendejano cannot heal, but we can fix. As people have come to worship things, some can only be reached by fixing their things. The healing is the part that comes after. It has to happen in their hearts."

Eugenio relaxed against the door frame, his schedule for the moment forgotten.

"I make my tools from what I find. My mornings are spent in the colossal dumps on the western edge of the city. In a different place, hundreds of birds would spend their days in The Dumps. For this reason, I've always found such places holy. But, here I am the only scavenger searching for preciousness."

She brought the recorder back down to her lap, pausing.

Eugenio roused himself and called out from the doorway.

"Goodbye, Lucine."

She turned, raised her hand goodbye.

At work, the heavy footfalls of battalion members' boots echoed down the central hallway of the Emergency Management Center just outside Eugenio's office. He sat at his narrow aluminum desk with the door open, lost for the moment in the distraction of the sound.

"Assem-ble!" someone yelled from further in the building. The footfalls receded in that direction.

Eugenio yawned as he stared at the reports on his tablet. The rank smell of the men and the insecticide they used shot down his throat, causing him to cough. He stood up and closed the door. He had let the routine reports pile up while he investigated more interesting aspects of the city's health, and now a full gig-disc's worth of work blinked red on his tablet, demanding attention. Some of the paperwork backlog had to be processed soon or someone would notice. He sighed and sat back down in his chair, mentally preparing himself for a long morning's slog. The sooner he cleared this work the sooner he could get back to tracking down Rory McClaren.

He would start with the entomological reports; though it was by no means his area of expertise, by virtue of necessity part of the caseload had been shunted off onto him. There just weren't enough entomologists on staff to handle the number of swarms and infestations that rippled through the city at an ever-increasing rate. Besides the recent rolling beetle incursion during the commemoration, a swarm of Africanized bees had attacked a transload of kids when the driver bumped into a hidden nest, causing a death and two hospitalizations.

So the bugs were once again a public relations priority, and thus nearly doubled the number of files waiting on Eugenio's review. The battalions would soon have to perform mass exterminations to keep both the populations in check—and then no doubt there would be another infestation next. The battalions might be meeting about that very fact right now, he thought. Swarms on the eastern side of the city had increased dramatically over the winter. Eugenio wondered just how much the city spent on the job that birds could easily perform. His finger hovered over the blinking red icon of the entomological reports and inched over to the opposite corner of the tablet where his most recent interview files were saved. He glanced up at the time and tapped that icon.

His interview with Dr. Etive booted up and began to play back, her voice clear and compelling in the quiet room. He jotted down notes as he listened: *conventioneers, carnivale tourists, costumes, virtu rigs, fighting, celebrities.*

"It's Rory McClaren. So you tell me."

Eugenio opened up the citizens' directory and typed in the name; a full page of links and references came up, but no physical address. He delved several layers into the information, up to the limit of his clearance until finally Eugenio found a record a quarter-century old: Penthouse, Spires, Building 1. Eugenio doubted it was still a valid address, but he had no other leads. With a last glance at the reports, Eugenio packed his bag and left the office bound for The Spires.

❖ ❖ ❖

Reaching into the stratus clouds, The Spires rose in front of Eugenio. The first two floors were encased in clear plexi. Through it he could see the building's waterfall and the sleek floating counters and seats from the street. His gaze lingered on the waterfall and slowly moved elsewhere. Above the first and second floor, the plexi reflected the surrounding buildings. The Spires, it seemed, had been designed to tantalize, but not to satisfy the desire of the onlooker—that was reserved for those permitted entrance, and not via the service entrances, Eugenio would wager.

On the other side of the plexi, a doorwoman approached the entrance and coded the visitor's portal down. As it separated from the plexi above it, a small line drew itself across the portal and descended a meter so that Eugenio could speak freely through the invisible barrier between him and the doorwoman.

"May I help you?" she asked.

"Yes, I'm here with the City Health Department." Eugenio held up his wrist for an ID scan.

As he expected, the door slid open even before he'd finished his last word. The doorwoman indicated the concierge's desk and went back to her post near the entrance. Eugenio approached the suited middle-aged man behind the counter. The suit must have cost as much as Eugenio's monthly pay.

"I need to speak with Rory McClaren." This brought the first sign of hesitation from the staff.

"Sir, The Spires' policy—"

"I'm not suggesting you let me into his home. Just the comm. Where is it?"

"Mr. McClaren does not receive visitors."

"I'm sure he can make an exception and receive one unannounced visitor."

"Excuse me, sir, but I didn't say unannounced visitors. I said visitors. Mr. McClaren does not receive visitors of any kind. Any exception would be by solely at Mr. McClaren's instruction."

"Listen—"

The concierge interrupted, speaking slowly. "Mr. McClaren has not left his residence, not once, since I have been employed here. I have recently celebrated my twentieth year with The Spires."

Eugenio blinked, considering this. It was only a momentary hesitation.

"Mr. . ." Eugenio began.

"Xiao," the concierge finished.

"Mr. Xiao, I'm sure I don't have to tell you that the City Health Department takes its responsibilities very seriously. Despite this, like any agency, mistakes are sometimes made. I have to admit that the City Health Department has neglected to do a full systems and residential inspection of The Spires in over—"

"The comms are right over here," Xiao said, directing him to a half-wall a few meters beyond the desk where he and Eugenio stood.

"If you please?" Xiao said, waving him closer. As Eugenio took two steps forward a half-moon of plexi swung out of nothingness and closed behind him.

"Mr. McClaren has unique protocols," Xiao explained. Eugenio waited as the other man input the code that would connect him to the penthouse. The line up to the penthouse rang audibly, a throwback Eugenio hadn't heard in years. On the fifth ring, Xiao turned to Eugenio.

"As I said, he's unaccustomed to visitors."

"Of course."

On the ninth ring, the line opened. There was no visual image to accompany the voice.

"Mr. McClaren, please excuse the intrusion. It's Nicholas from Personal Relations. There's a Dr. Eugenio Oliveira from the Emergency Management Division of the City Health Department here to speak with you, sir."

Silence from the other end.

"I'll leave you two. If you need anything, sir, don't hesitate to call," Xiao said. He walked toward the plexi until it gave way, and stepped deftly out of the small booth.

"Mr. McClaren?" Eugenio asked uncertainly.

A strong, slow voice filled up the booth. "I've no business with the City Health Department. A contact person has been assigned for all administrative affairs; it's in the records. I suggest you get in touch with him. Good—"

"Mr. McClaren, thank you for taking the time to speak to me, but I'm not here on an administrative matter. I'm researching the Crumble epidemic."

Silence. Eugenio continued.

"I recently conducted an interview with Dr. Rosalynn Etive, and she mentioned that she and her husband had been with you on the night that the news of the infection began to spread. I'd very much like to speak with you in order to get your impressions and memories of that time."

No response came.

"Mr. McClaren, I assure you I wouldn't waste your time if this weren't a very important matter. I don't have to tell you how much was lost—"

"No, you certainly don't."

"Getting your impressions would be tremendously helpful."

"All that's done now," came the voice on the other end. The connection was severed.

7

Rory wouldn't share those days with anyone. He hadn't then and he wouldn't now. Who was this Eugenio Oliveira to try and call him down from his tower? Rory leaned against the kitchen counter, trying to catch his breath, his thoughts, and a break from the onslaught of guilt that began to press down on him. He had survived, but was this what he had survived for?

He looked around his empty rooms and beyond them out into the city teeming with life, just a few centimeters of plexi separating him. Or was it teeming with death and danger? Rory couldn't be sure anymore. The world was a memory and when not that, a show he watched in his living room, but not much more. He struggled to take a breath. Rory left the great room and entered his bedroom; the softness of the grass underfoot soothed his skin, traveled up and tried to penetrate his thoughts. By the time he reached his armoire he'd begun to feel a bit better, but he knew the contents of the bag inside would calm him.

The black leather satchel contained an innoculator, new hearing aids, credit stick, palmlock, keys, reconsti food, flash light, water purification tablets, a rainbow of antibiotics and supplement tablets, GPS, a battalion-grade retractable stun stick disguised as a cane, and of course a portable virtu rig and recorder. Rory called it an emergence kit. He had inherited his Pop Pop's sense of humor. As much as he wanted to use the kit, he doubted he ever would; the time was never right to leave, what with so many people between him and home. Still, he checked the contents on Thursdays and reordered supplies each quarter, regular as Leiodare's unremarkable seasons. He'd toyed with the idea of being buried with it—one way or another, some day he and it would get out of these rooms together.

8

The Dire lived up to its name. Everywhere Anna looked a profusion of people, carts, signs and storefronts vied for her attention in the narrow streets. From building to building the smells assaulted her—first garlic rolling out of a restaurant, then blood at a scarification parlor, urine in an alleyway, the rich smell of honeysuckle at the herbalist, and burning hair at the beauty shop that abutted it.

The intensity of the place was well known to locals and tourists. Because of The Dire's reputation for feeding on the uninitiated, trans usually parked at the edges and only a few tourists were brave enough to venture more than a couple of blocks in. Battalions even avoided the place as much as possible. So here at the esoteric center where Anna now found herself, Leiodare's shadow economy was on full display. As she made her way to Leiodare's largest virtu nexus, The White Light, live bird calls from illegal stalls punctuated the din. She looked around and saw a woman pull back the drape on a cage. A bright green parakeet stood inside.

"Wild lured," she called out to Anna. "From a hole in the perimeter."

"There are no holes in the perimeter," cried the cart owner next to her. "The bird's raised, sure as you are."

"How would you know?" the peddler squawked back. Anna hurried on as the woman tried to lock gazes with her.

Up ahead, the building came into view—an aluminum facade with holo hawkers out front shouting the nexus's wares. Anna ducked in, from one crush of humanity to the next.

Inside the dim nexus, soft lights highlighted the attractions in the main hall. Anna's gaze followed the spotlights, searching. A bank of booths made up one side of the room. Judging by the huge, unwieldy rigs that hung from them, Anna supposed they must be early models of virtu. For the moment they were empty, but as she watched a man entered the one farthest from her and put the rig over his head, inserting a token into a slot. His face went slack as the real began.

Beyond these booths Anna saw a jukebox-like server and a hallway with several private rooms, similar to the ones that she and Peru had often used to review their virtu reals before they set a final price. Nearest her stood a long line of partitions separated by plexi walls coated with simulating foam that intermittently moved closer to the users, embracing the half-dozen people in each cell to enhance whatever sensation their mind saw behind the blacked glasses of their virtu rigs. In the center of the room another twenty or so people were seated at a sort of massive lazy Susan studded with virtu rigs.

The White Light brought back Anna's old mixed feelings about the time she and Peru had spent recording reals to get by. Suppressing those feelings, she looked around the room for an attendant to whom she could speak to about any new exceptional reals. Peru's work wouldn't be found in any of these arcade attractions next to teenage threesomes and lunar walks. There was no front desk or call button; Anna wasn't sure where she should look for the attendant. She walked around the corner and saw only private rooms. She walked to the end of the hallway where a group of forty or more people all looked to be linked into the same real. Clothes started to come off. Anna turned around, intending to go back the way she'd come. A girl, perhaps thirteen years old, stood in front of her, dressed in black leggings and t-shirt. She wore large, beat-up red work boots with the tongues pulled out through the laces.

"Need something?" the girl asked.

Anna furrowed her brow; she looked up the hall to see if there was anyone else.

"You're looking for someone—probably me. Do you need a real?" The girl chuckled at the look on Anna's face. "I work here. I'm the attendant. You're looking for me, right?"

Anna answered slowly, her brain still resisting this possibility.

"Yes, I guess I was."

"What do you need?"

The girl kept using that word. Anna didn't like the conclusion it contained. Still, she had to admit she'd been compelled to come here—just not for the reason the girl assumed.

"I'm looking for something exceptional."

"What's your exceptional? We've got surgery, sex, crime, transmutation—"

"Anything from Peru?"

"We don't usually break it up by place, I'll have to look."

"No, from Peru, the virtuoso. Anything branded Lima or Quito?"

The girl's eyes narrowed and she nodded appreciatively. "You know her work. You're a connoisseur then? She had a piece once where—"

"Do you have any?" Anna asked.

"It would cost."

"I have money. Do you have a new real?"

"The piece that she had it was a stereo feed, you know I'm sure, the ones with two virtuosos doing a simultaneous record. But this one was much better than any others. The other virtuoso was the only one nearly as good as her. Her handle was Armour, but she stopped recording a couple of years back. That real, though there was something about their frequencies, made it the best jack ever. There are harmonics, these beautiful bits of emotions and images that weren't there, you know, like not in the world, but only created because of these two. Incredible shit. Hasn't been anything like it before or since."

Anna glared at the girl, and had to look down lest she notice.

"That real set off a fire. Everyone wanted them and zzzt they both disappeared. Like legends. People tried to track them down—they'd let slip a clue. That virtuoso, her handle had always been Quito but in the real, the other said a different name. I'd almost forgotten what it was, but you must have seen the real, 'cause it was Peru, right?"

The cold dread that crept up Anna's spine since the girl began the story stopped just above her shoulders.

"Yes," Anna said. With a conscious effort she made her tone sound casual. "It was Peru. That real, that's the kind of thing I'm trying to find. Have anything like that?"

"Oh, everyone started using those names after that—Titicaca, Piura, Chachapoya, Moyobamba. She became impossible to track after that."

"Yes, I know," Anna said, almost to herself. "I was hoping you might know more or come across one of her reals since then."

"Nothing. And the other one, who knows? Just dropped off into space somewhere. But—we do have some amazing stuff coming out of Budapest."

"No. Thanks," Anna said, brushing past the girl and toward the exit.

As Anna made her way back through The Dire's maze, she found her past around every corner, her regrets and reminiscences waiting in the shadows.

The afternoon that her mother died, Anna was to join Bly downtown after her mother finished a business meeting. It was meant to have been a planning afternoon; thoughts were jammed up to the edges of Anna's skull—how to get into the

coveted Sloan Arts Academy, ways to save for a cross-coun-
try trip, when she'd have to start. Anna waited at a fountain
for her mother. It was a bright day brimming with color, and
Anna itched to be home with her oils and pastels or even for
a holo pad so she could render the saturated afternoon light
as vibrantly as it shone. Maybe she could include it in her
admission application, she thought.

Out of the corner of her eye she watched her mother fin-
ishing up her goodbyes in an adjacent courtyard. Anna knew
Bly had been pitching her reintroduction campaign to a group
of investors. Bly had gone over the speech so many times that
Anna felt certain she could read her lips from afar as Bly reiter-
ated key points. Anna watched her mother wrangle the group
toward her desired result, and gracefully turn to exit.

For years after, Anna racked her brain to see if she'd suspected anything about the woman jogging by, the one who wore
a yellow jumper and bare legs. Over the years Anna embellished
her with details: a staggered gait to her step, freckles, a scar on
her knee, sometimes a ring, but really she didn't remember
the woman clearly. She'd been just a momentary hiccup in her
mother's goodbyes. The jogger had bumped into Bly, mumbled
an apology and sprinted down the block before anyone realized
what had happened.

After the collision, Bly briefly looked confused and clutched
at the inner pocket of her jacket. She turned towards Anna,
locked onto her gaze and then doubled over and hit the ground.
The circle of investors stepped back, but a second later hovered
closer, as blood began to pool on the ground beneath Bly. They
asked questions, but didn't contact with her.

Anna was the first to touch her mother, the only one before
the paramedics arrived. She cradled Bly's head in her lap and
stroked her forehead, fighting the panic that welled up in her
chest. A few breaths after her mother dropped, Anna began to
follow instructions. They issued from somewhere inside her,

a combination of memory and survival, everything Bly had taught her and developed her to discern, repeated itself calmly and quietly until Anna obeyed—*Put her head in your lap, say the right things. Don't panic. Stay here with her. See her there in her eyes, tell her yes, tell her you remember. Listen. Tell her—. She's not breathing anymore, she's not breathing, she's not—. She won't be breathing again. Stand up, Anna, walk away. Put that back. Fine, keep it safe then. Keep it close. Stand up, Anna.*

Walk away.

She had kept walking until she reached their home. She'd made it as far as closing their front door, before she collapsed with Bly's bloody jacket clutched to her chest. A meter away, on a table, Bly's credit stick blinked green as Anna stared, still unable to form a single thought. There was only the knot of horror and grief that occupied her chest. When the first tear dropped onto her shirt, it touched the tight ball of pain that had hit her the moment Bly had hit the ground. It expanded, decompressed and the pain broke open in her chest. In the process, she lost several hours.

Anna found herself in the studio, sprawled on the floor in front of a large, raised platform. Remnants of wax caked the top of it. Thick stalagmites of the stuff stuck up at the edges of the platform. Dapples of blood speckled the side nearest Anna. She got her legs beneath her, noticing tiny cuts on her ankles and on one hand between the index finger and thumb. Her back ached as she stood. A bit unsteady on her feet, Anna studied the platform, trying to piece together the time that had been lost and place what she was looking at. She leaned over to get a better look and quickly drew back, unable to catch her breath.

Two footprints, slightly larger than her own, clearly stood in the wax, a few centimeters apart. And behind them she saw the unmistakable impression of buttocks.

What have you done?

Anna's gaze followed the trail of wax crackles, thin as shavings, that led from the platform, across the room, and to the window. There the glass had been broken out; a single triangle of it remained in one corner. Anna found herself staring at the fire escape.

She's gone. But you can find her. You can bring her back. This one you can bring back.

Anna stood staring, unable even to move.

You'll find her, but now you have to go. You have to hide. Disappear, Anna. Go.

On that night, Anna did what the voice told her to, took what she needed and walked away from their home, into the woods. Wandering alone, she remembered those lost hours—not what she'd been thinking when she did it or how it felt. She remembered what she saw—*that* she could be certain of, that she knew.

She knew that the woman had been beautiful in the light. Anna had stood centimeters from the platform watching her flow into the form that Anna had sculpted. It took no more than a few minutes for her to emerge. The wax turned brackish, darkest in the center and all else flowed from there, a network of veins and capillaries crackled their way throughout the wax. Actual arms grew inside the sculpted ones, and legs lengthened inside the wax shell. For a breath all movement stopped and Anna stepped closer, awed by what she saw. The overhead lamp made the woman's skin glisten through the thin layer of wax that covered her. Anna could do no more than stare, her nose almost touching the other's.

The woman was born with her eyes open. Her first breath cracked the wax that covered her. With her second breath, she screamed. Anna remembered being knocked off her feet and the sight of the woman, terrified and half-naked, Bly's bloodied jacket covering all but her legs, as she ran across the room, bumped into the frame of the window. And crashed through the glass. Shards of it rained down to the floor, shattering and shooting in all directions. Afterwards, Anna lay in the aftermath, grasping for a thought.

Even in the woods, Anna's daze would not lift, but some part of her remained alert. Only the voice maintained control, guiding her to rest and walk. That close to home, the woods were artificial, a carbon exchange environment meant to allay the guilt of distant city-states as they continued to chop and burn at will. Winding her way through the maze of saplings only added to the surreal quality Anna's life had taken on. She had no family or friends. Bly had taught her that trusting could be dangerous, that she should be able to trust herself and if need be, only herself.

So Anna wandered for months, her only companion a small crystal radio she'd made with her mother's guidance. It had been her first inorganic creation. Oddly it had been more of a challenge than the animals and plants—not just because of the poisonous galena and other dangerous elements, but because things didn't have a feel, just a set of rules to follow. Her creativity couldn't help her.

She had overcome the challenge, to her mother's delight—creating first the detector and then the tuning coil. After a brief rest she produced the earphones in one whole piece. Just to watch Bly smile, Anna had replicated the long antennae wire slowly winding it around a diamond-shaped frame until it resembled a kite. The kite antennae peeked out of the top of her pack as she walked through the woods. It still picked up twenty-two of the twenty-four stations that had once filled their home with syncopated rhythms, late-night recitations, pulsar plays, and time-delayed music festivals from outlying colonies.

Out amongst the long shadows and over-populated warrens of the woods, the radio provided Anna's only comfort. Pulsar plays still dominated the hours between 22:00 and

23:00. If she had had the desire she could still shake her hips to 633's rumba hop hour, but no such desire remained. The background of her life remained in place even if the foreground had shifted drastically.

She rented rooms in bamboo motels so she could sit on their respective balconies and stare into space while mosquitoes beat against the netting that separated her from what lurked beyond. Always she kept moving.

Walking from town to town, her baby fat fell away, her hair became unkempt. But she still showered daily, memories of her mother's voice in her ear, "Anna, please, some things are meant to be pristine. You're one of them."

Somewhere in the middle of the woods the radio stopped working: no more plays or recitations, no more rhythms to block out thought. Dark circles appeared under Anna's eyes. Her gaze twitched from tree to tree until exhausted, she had to remind herself to stay alert, not to stare at her feet or at anyone with anything but certainty.

Eventually the woods became a forest that gave through to a jungle with wide lanes carved below the canopy. There, trundlers and touristies filled with mild-mannered adventurers hovered above the undergrowth, recording their current hermetic travels for later viewing on even milder days. Anna avoided the crowds to find a more isolated path. She was running out of options and she feared that the anxiety in her expression would be all too readable for the opportunists who populated the jungle towns.

Bly's credit stick had gone from mellow pulsing green to an insistent red blinking and soon would go dead altogether. Anna had to do something and only one option seemed remotely palatable. After all, she told herself, doing virtually objectionable things still beat doing actual ones. Anna knew that she would have to become a virtuoso; it was just a matter of when.

On the day after she ate her last pack of reconsti food, Anna walked straight into the center of an outpost to find the highest bidder. The outpost was an outdated electro town, Gene, with a few cars that still ran on gas ambling through the streets. Above them, tubes of neon spelled out slogans to touristies and passersby—a town sure to have virtu trade. She need only find the brightest lights, the loudest music and Anna was sure she could find someone to pay her to produce a real. She just hoped it would be the kind of real she could agree to do. Bly would not approve, but even her mother's approval had become a luxury.

Once Bly had been excited by virtu. She'd spent weeks talking about the possibilities that kind of technology opened up. But by the time Anna was fourteen, she'd warned her away from it. Of all the vices available, virtu, her mother had told her was the worst. The idea of neurologically recording one's experiences and selling them to another to be played back while linked straight into the brain was not foreign to Anna. She'd grown up with the stories all over the Net, with shops dedicated to the sale of virtu reals, online sites that sold cut-rate packs good for a permanent blank stare and not much else. For Anna, virtu was as omnipresent as any other welcome distraction. Bly came to despise everything about it.

"They make it sound good, Anna, but it's not safe. People have lost their lives—trading them in and some just lost them altogether. Virtuoso used to mean something, something of substance," Bly had said with visible disgust.

The name wasn't particularly fitting to many of the actions typically recorded on a real. But sometimes it took a bit of extra stroking to get someone to walk up to a black bear and, once there, not faint when the true size of its claws registered in the part of the mind that's called upon to slow down the perception of time at such moments—this so that one seems to live longer than the few seconds that follow.

Anna would not face any black bears she knew, but she would have to face her mother's fear and not to lose herself in the process.

Making her way through the center of the outpost, Anna walked toward the bright edge of town. Just as she suspected, people peppered the streets there, each one standing a short distance from the next, waiting for customers. There were a disproportionate number of kids—both girls and boys—and other people whom she could only describe as broken. Tossed about by some unknown current, they had all washed up here with only their brains and bodies left to trade for the necessities.

Uncertain of how to begin, Anna walked the line, stealing looks at and around the virtuosos, trying to search out someone who might be in charge, one who might be looking to add another to a group of contractors.

At the end of the line, a cheerful man wearing silk pajamas approached her and offered to buy her a cool refresca. Anna averted her eyes and hurried to the end of the block. A person stood at the corner leaning against the last building, a café. In her haste, Anna almost ran straight into her. It was a woman leaning, one hand supporting her weight with her head down. She wore a pair of blackout shades. Anna stood there, clothes sweated through, the beginning of a wildness in her eyes, and a stun stick gripped tightly in her hand.

When the woman looked up, Anna took an unconscious step away, not sure if her mind was deceiving her. The woman from the wax stood gaping at her with the same disbelief that Anna felt. Freed from the wax, her face was more beautiful than Anna had remembered though she had acquired a short jagged scar on her jaw. The woman reached up to the temple of the shades she wore and pushed a small button as yet unseen by Anna. Anna watched the glasses give a bit where she touched them. The woman took the shades off quickly, folded them and stowed them in the black flack vest she wore, all the while continuing to stare at Anna.

Anna took a cautious step forward. She leaned the top half of her body forward, feeling pulled in that direction. Anna saw a pretty young woman with an earnest face who seemed neither a threat nor a mirage. She didn't look a thing like Bly, to Anna's relief. The realization brought a faint question up in her mind but there were too many thoughts to give it any attention. The woman wore a black shirt beneath the flak vest, and heavy blue pants tucked into careworn worker's boots. Anna was not so woodswise, more seed than tree, and certainly no root, so she didn't recognize the gear that the woman wore: the telltale dark shades and thin black wire that led to an as-yet-unseen virtu recorder in the vest. Anna's voice shook, but she spoke first.

"Hello. My name is Anna Armour."

The woman retreated a step away from her as she surveyed the plane of Anna's face from forehead to lips.

"How did you find me?" the woman asked.

Her voice sounded older than Anna's. In fact she looked older—perhaps twenty for Anna's fifteen years. And it wasn't quite the response Anna had been hoping for, but to hear anyone answer at all—anyone outside of her own head—relieved some of the pressure that had been building inside her. Her hopes of ever finding the woman had dimmed to a glimmer and now after nearly a year she'd not been at all what Anna expected. She would have had trouble distinguishing the woman from anyone else she'd seen in the last several months. If anything the woman seemed healthier than the other people Anna had encountered. She had so many questions, but she knew she must let her take her time and share later. This was not Ms. Janks.

The woman stood squared off, her feet planted as wide as her angled shoulders. Almost a fighting stance, Anna thought, though her expression looked less certain than her body.

"I didn't find you," Anna responded, "I think you found me. What." Anna blinked. "What is your name?"

This seemed to appease the woman. She looked away, relaxed her shoulders. She said, "You can call me Peru."

"Ah, Peru. Perhaps I can buy you both a drink?" a stranger's voice called from behind them. Anna turned to find the man in the silk pajamas standing a few meters away, smiling broadly. A soft breeze lifted the front of his shirt up to reveal wiry patches of hair covering his considerable girth.

Peru agreed and turned to the café with the man, leaving Anna to stay behind for a few seconds and consider what to do. By the time she'd joined them at a small table in the café, they were already in negotiations.

"My work is good," Peru had said.

"You're building a reputation." The man had glanced up at Anna. "This one too?"

Peru's jaw hardened momentarily, but she continued on, a slight edge in her voice. The virtu negotiations turned to Peru's favor and Anna only half-listened. For the moment she was dumbfounded—by the nature of the negotiations as well as who sat next to her.

But the next time that the silk-pajamaed man offered to buy them a drink, a week later, Anna answered first. Shortly after, they made their way to the open-air restaurant that would become their meeting place whenever the girls came to town. He still spoke to Peru almost exclusively. Anna told herself it was because Peru looked older. But eventually he offered Anna her first job. Peru asked if he had any more work, something simple she said, looking over at Anna.

"Your name?"

"Armour, Anna Armour." She knew enough to lie, but when the question was posed to her she'd forgotten what she was supposed to say. She grimaced and answered again.

"Armour, just Armour."

"I might have something for you. Can you swim?"

"Yes," she replied.

"Good. Your client cannot, but he wants to participate in this year's Epiphany. You'll do it for him. Just pretend to be Greek Orthodox—and a boy. You can do that, can't you?"

She could. She didn't retrieve the cross that the priest had flung into the water. She hung back in her dinghy for fear that even in the huge crowd of participants she'd be found out for who she was in the white T-shirt and frigid water, but she satisfied the contract and the customer. She had earned enough money to pay for the next two days at the motel and recharge the credit stick to a pale green. She could even pay for her very own recorder—an overly large second-generation affair, but it beat borrowing Peru's. They could now make money at the same time, and perhaps even work together. As it turned out they rarely had the opportunity—in the end they worked on very different jobs.

Anna's first real had gone so well that the client requested her again. This time for a long luxurious swim out on the river. Apparently the real was his effort to help overcome a fear of drowning the agent told her. In a few weeks she already had a specialization: Anna handled surrogacies. All virtu work was rooted in surrogate sensations, but surrogacies in particular focused on walking for the wounded, seeing for the newly blind, dancing for the hopeless, doing what someone truly could not do—not just what they feared to do. Those assignments went to Peru.

"Truly virtuous," Peru would call Anna's work, her tone indecipherable. At first Peru had passed the work on to Anna. It didn't pay well, she said, but Anna suspected Peru wanted to protect her from the other jobs.

"You'd just mess them up," Peru would say, but Anna knew differently.

After a few months, clients requested Anna by name, wanted "Armour" to swim for them, to climb their mountains.

Peru continued to risk for her reward, facing other people's fears and often their fetishes. The work wore on Peru. One late afternoon, Anna came back to the motel room to find Peru gone. Anna thought that perhaps she'd had another overnight assignment. She had them often enough, but Peru always gave Anna advance notice and frequently checked in on her while she was away. This time, nothing. For three days Anna waited—for a response to her messages or for Peru to come back. On the fourth night, Peru's key in the lock woke Anna from sleep and she ran to her.

Anna never asked where Peru had been; she was too thrilled that Peru had returned. Still something continued to plague Peru. To Anna, she would only speak of the work.

"They're selling my memories," Peru said.

"But not your actual memories, not from your actual life," Anna replied.

"I'm the one doing them, virtu pack or no. They're my reactions, my sight, my life they're selling. I did those things, not them."

"But still they don't have what you do when you're not wearing the pack."

Peru didn't answer that line of reasoning. Whether because it poked a hole in her argument or not Anna couldn't be sure. Because of it, Anna couldn't help wondering if Peru took the gear off when she came to her that night.

She had reached up to take off Peru's shades and Peru stopped her hand.

"It's too bright without them," Peru had said.

"You don't need to see. I'm right here. You can feel it," Anna answered.

Peru had exhaled brusquely and not moved one centimeter, only looked down at Anna until she started to feel uncomfortable with the intensity of her gaze.

Too quickly, she had acquiesced, and opened to Peru's hands, letting the power of their good times persuade her.

She had never planned on making love to Peru and in truth she didn't; Peru took charge as was her nature, leaving Anna lying in the aftermath, guilty and satisfied, twisted by feelings that drove her out of the bed and out into the stand of trees outside the motel they'd been staying in. The feeling didn't fit inside her. She knew it would soon spill out and for that at least she wanted solitude. A couple of men sat smoking and talking near the door, so Anna moved further into the foliage. She watched the orange tips of their cigars, the beginning of a chill setting in, unable to form a clear thought.

She couldn't articulate the tangle that rose up in her. There had always been something unnameable between them. For years, including the two that they were together and more so all those they spent apart, Anna could not fully understand it. She should have been the one who taught Peru about the world, instead of having to find her after she had learned cruel, unspoken lessons, who should have found a way for them to survive, who should have led.

Anna wondered if Peru had made love to her that night so that Anna would miss her more after she left. She could almost understand why she would do such a thing. The grief with which she had created Peru must have left the other woman missing something. Peru had always insinuated it, and Anna knew she had sculpted her out of desperation as much as wax and drops of her mother's blood.

❖ ❖ ❖

The morning after they made love, Peru had taken Anna deep into the jungle.

"This is a sacred place," Peru had said, looking out on the barren stretch of land she and Anna had trekked two days through dense brush to visit. It looked to Anna like an empty lot, a mistake in the middle of jungle that nature forgot to fill in, and considering how quickly the jungle usually reclaimed space, the emptiness dismayed Anna as quickly as a pimp on a street corner looking her way. She felt in violation of some unspoken rule, as though she shouldn't be standing at there though she had every right.

Peru took a few steps away from her, striding further onto the empty land. She swiveled her head back and forth, taking in Anna had no idea what. Anna waited for her to continue.

"Why is it sacred?" Anna asked.

"I found my way here," Peru looked at Anna, a strange expression on her face—a half smirk with a defiant eyebrow. She had searched Anna's face for a reaction. When none came, Peru continued.

"I found my way here, after that first night. And last year, I found my way here again. The Mendejano perform first rites here. As a way of fixing this land after the pharmas laid it to waste," she said.

"First rites?" Anna'd asked, and so had begun Peru's one and only divulgence of information. She never talked about her time alone, before or after that day they met in Gene. When they were together, Peru interacted freely. She acted as if they were the couple they appeared to be and went out of her way to make Anna laugh. But when she went off on her own for hours, and occasionally a day or two for an assigned real, those times were well-guarded secrets.

But that day Peru talked about those she called her family, saying more than she had in all the time that they knew each other. Much later Anna learned the reason for the sudden openness. It was Peru's day of confession, as close to a Mendejano holiday as Anna was likely to experience. Until then she hadn't known that Peru had a faith, or anything about the times that Peru drifted away.

Peru carefully laid the contents of their packs at the edge of the clearing. She took each item out slowly and painstakingly placed each one so that it created the shape of a circle.

"This is the inner circle," Peru said. She continued. "Objects have the power to create change. But most people have gotten it wrong. They can't make you a better person or happier in and of themselves. Every object is a tool."

Anna peered at Peru, trying to decipher her meaning.

"So this leaf?" Anna asked.

Peru nodded. "Yes, a tool."

"What can it do?" Anna asked.

"It can make you see beauty. It can hide what's beautiful—the bird in a tree, for example," Peru said, pulling back a branch on a nearby tree.

Anna still couldn't dispel her confusion; she felt a further distance opening between them.

"It's all about what you can make out of what you have. Isn't that right?" Peru had looked at her pointedly.

It was the first time she'd said anything about being created. Peru didn't speak of it again until months after that day, and even then it came out sideways. She had just received an offer for an assignment at twice what she'd once been paid for the same fantasy. Still Peru had seemed less than pleased and Anna saw her opportunity.

"Maybe it's time to quit. We could do more harvesting," Anna said. "I mean we're seventeen now."

"You are seventeen," Peru said from the bed where she sat.

Heat flushed Anna's face but she continued. "—And we have money. We could move somewhere permanent, maybe go to school."

"I can't go to school, Anna. I have no records."

"We can get records anywhere in this town for less credits than a nice meal. You know that."

"I don't need school. I learn quickly," Peru said, looking at Anna steadily. "And why would I want to stop? Virtu has been good to me. It took care of me when there was nothing else."

"How did—" Anna began. Peru glared at her, and she again abandoned that line of questioning.

"You've no idea what can happen to a girl alone out there," Peru said.

"I've some idea," Anna replied. Peru ignored her.

"Besides, they say I'm very good at it. Clean slate and all," Peru replied sharply. There was a warning in her tone Anna heeded it. Peru exhaled slowly and turned her whole body to Anna.

"Why?" Peru asked.

Finally, she had asked. Anna turned and faced Peru, surprised to see tears in her eyes. The edgy expression remained.

"I—I don't know," Anna said. Peru regarded her with contempt.

"You don't know why you made me?"

"I was terrified. In shock. Arrogant. I don't know, Peru. I don't know what you want me to say. I did it and I can't undo it." She gestured to Peru. "Look at you. You're amazing. Beautiful, strong, better at life than I am, I think. Certainly tougher. You're a fighter. You're the best—"

"—thing that you've ever done," Peru finished.

"You know I wasn't going to say that."

Peru grunted and walked over to Anna, stopped when they were nose to nose and said, "You just didn't want to be alone."

With that she left the room, slamming the door behind her.

Peru didn't return until much later that night. The front door to the room crashed open, leaving a dent in the wall behind it. As it crept back on its hinges, Peru entered. Leaves stuck out of her hair at odd angles. Mud covered her clothes; a jagged hole had been ripped in the leg of her pants.

Anna watched warily from the bathroom doorway as Peru dragged over to her—she smelled of rank river water—and stopped a meter in front of her. Peru reached out to the virtu pack on the dresser and went to put it on Anna. Anna started to back away and Peru quieted her with a look. It said *Do this, now, or. . .* Anna didn't wait for *or*; she closed her eyes and waited for

Peru to affix the shades and the light skull-frame. Anna heard the small power surge right before Peru hit "Play".

Though Anna's eyes remained closed behind the shades, she saw the trees just outside the motel. She recognized the water fixture near the parking lot and the front door of their own room as the perspective shifted to look behind her. The visual perspective was incredibly fluid. Anna had had to jack in a few times to learn how to make better reals—to look more slowly, to shut out her own thoughts as much as possible, to be in the moment. Both she and Peru excelled at the work because of what must have been heightened sensitivity. All their customers had come back for more because of the power of their reals.

Experiencing Peru's perspective, Anna understood the attraction: the other woman's senses exuded an intensity that felt more powerful than her own because nothing seemed dulled. As the real's perspective moved into the more populated portions of the town, she saw the world with a newness that felt like pleasure—a completeness Anna didn't think she was still capable of feeling. The sky seemed brighter, smells more complex. Peru's senses took nothing for granted and fully absorbed her environment, before categorizing it, dismissing it—if they ever dismissed it at all. Her perspective almost suspended time as each sensation was devoured and cast aside for the next.

Even with all this Anna keenly felt another difference: Peru's thoughts weren't removed from this real, nor were her feelings or her fears. Underneath the newness, Peru felt oddly disconnected. Her gaze settled on a tree for the same amount of time as a person—man or woman, near or far, speaking to her or not. Not only that, but she felt the same way about all of them—nothing received special attention or a second look. Almost as if Peru had no reaction to the world at all because the reaction to everything was the same—an unrelenting fascination.

Anna followed Peru's perspective as she walked around to the motel they were staying in. She skirted the front door and went around to the bathroom window. She tried to peer in, but the plexi was shaded. She went round to the other side and looked into the kitchenette where Anna came into view sitting on the living room couch. Seeing herself unnerved her and only with a conscious effort did she keep the shades on.

Once her own panic passed she felt odd sensations. Waves of emotion hit her, but she could not sort them out. Apprehension, longing, rage, attachment. Nothing quite like love or heavy as hate when Peru looked at Anna, but it lay weighty and full—just beyond her recognition. Everything she felt, she only seemed to feel at Anna. And it seemed to her it made Peru as uncomfortable as the thought of it made her. The past-tense Anna, the one who Peru watched, stood and crossed the room to the window. She pulled the shade back a few centimeters, no doubt looking for Peru. Anna remembered that she had been wondering if Peru would come back. Anna felt longing in her chest, not sure if the feeling were hers or Peru's.

Peru's perspective walked into the woods that surrounded the motel, her gaze trained on the ground. Not far from the motel room where they were staying, she stopped and dropped down. The real's perspective lowered and settled on a tiny white skeleton partially obscured by tufts of grass. Anna couldn't tell what it had been—perhaps a newt or gecko. Peru closed her hand around the skeleton, and Anna began to feel uneasy. When Peru opened her hand, a light brown lizard scurried off of it.

A bolt of panic shot through Anna.

The real went black.

"Peru, you can't show your gift. They'll find—" Anna began, pulling off the shades.

She saw an empty room. She looked behind her, into the bathroom. Peru's toiletries were missing. As her gaze traveled around the room she saw that Peru's clothes had been taken from the closet; the bag with all her virtu gear no longer sat at the foot of the bed; even the food that had been on the counter was no longer there.

Peru had left nothing but Anna behind.

❖ ❖ ❖

Now, as Anna sat at home in the giene spa, sketching with her back against the tub, the cygnets kept her company. The bag and coat she'd worn to The Dire were tumbling through the dry cycle in the other room. Every few seconds the sound of her belt hitting the side of the dryer rang out.

Anna drew a nearly perfect oval, indiscernible from any other oval, but one that she knew was an egg, even before she sketched the nest, the thin branch, a patch of cloud behind it. As she finished the rounded edge of a distant leaf, the egg started to rise from the paper. Anna cupped her hands around the space and cradled it as it finished emerging. The egg felt fragile in her hands, as if a breath could crack it.

She placed the egg in her lap and looked around the room for some place to rest it, not wanting to move. There was nothing. Anna removed her shirt and shaped it into a makeshift nest. The tub's cold pricked her skin as she brushed against it, leaning over to place the nest next to her. She placed the egg inside the nest.

Anna scooted her back down the tub's porcelain, starting at each touch of cold. She leaned her head back until it touched the lip of the tub. Letting her gaze drift to the side, she watched the cygnets floating serenely, but from the smell, she knew the tub would have to be cleaned again soon. It must have set off a sensor in the lights; they glowed more brightly than usual, hurting her eyes when she looked up. Squinting, Anna looked back down at the floor where the egg sat in the T-shirt nest next to her.

She should make a package to replace the parcels she'd left behind at the club. She still had a fountain pen and digi of king music she hadn't sent. For the first time, she wondered why. In all the years she'd been trying to contact Peru she'd only ever received one response: "There's nothing to say." So Anna had stopped trying to say anything, and began sending the packages. They weren't gifts. She thought certainly they were the only thing Peru might understand, their only chance at communication. After all, Peru had taught her about the power of objects.

She abandoned her sketch pad and went out to the living room.

Anna stood alone, shirtless, in the dim lights of her darkened apartment. She hoped that the package she sent would be a tool and work its magic. After she loaded the items into the box, she carefully drew three small green stars on the top right corner and initialed it as she always did.

9

The McClaren dead end had led Eugenio back to his careworn station at the archives of the City Health Department. After he left The Spires, he'd briefly considered doing a follow-up interview with Dr. Etive, but without any new information there was no point. He had to be missing something. He had no alternative but to go back over the files and broaden his perspective.

He loaded up the city reports and files from December thirtieth. Resigned, Eugenio sighed and began slowly scrolling through City Health's official report. He began to recite it by heart within a few sentences and stopped. Pinching the bridge of his nose, he closed his eyes and looked down at the polished table in front of him. The place smelled of stale air and boredom.

Every city report would be this way, Eugenio knew; he feared that every document in the archives that related to the Crumble might be. He'd spent not just the four years of his professional life researching the topic, but both his public health and anthropology academic careers were centered on some aspect. His familiarity, Eugenio knew, could be his downfall. His mind followed along the same overused tracks, and though his interviews inspired him to look at new parts of the terrain, the country was still too familiar. He'd have to try something else.

Frustrated, he took out his tablet to link up to the Net. He hoped some free-associative phrase searches would help him come up with some new tactics. The screensaver was the view of a particular peak he and Lucine had summited last year. He smiled at the memory of Lucine chastising him for using the word.

"We climbed a hill, Eu. That's all. No reason to make up words."

"But a picture is worth a thousand words," he'd replied. He'd come across the phrase in a twenty-first-century lit course and it'd stuck with him. He repeated it again, under his breath, smiling at the memory.

"A picture is worth a thousand words."

Eugenio laid the tablet back down on the desk and turned back to the reader.

"Open images, labeled 'Crumble', 'epidemic', 'quarantine'. ICDC quarantine period. Slideshow."

Visual horrors paraded before his eyes. Without thinking he began to chew the tip of his index finger. One of the images was an iconic one from that time. He'd seen it dozens of times—in his own schoolbooks and specials on national broadcasts. In it, a young girl stands next to a body, with a vulture perched where the head should be, its beak half into what had once been a face. The girl wails, horrified and frozen. Looking at it, the skin on Eugenio's arms began to tingle and a swell of anxiety rose from the pit of his stomach up through his diaphragm. His vision began to tunnel.

Eugenio closed the file and tried to take a deep breath. Not again: it had been at least a year since the last attack and its return wasn't welcomed. He thought the exposure treatments had been working—though he only exposed himself to photos, but something about the brutality of that particular image triggered all the old fears.

He reopened the image, and immediately felt nauseated. He made himself go to the next image and the next, his finger hovering over the "next" button, clicking through as his discomfort ratcheted up. There: a murder of crows perched just above a group of people sleeping in the Gardens. At least he hoped they were sleeping. Again: another group of birds indifferent to the man curled up on the ground. In another, a flock of white-headed pigeons feasting on a fruit cart while meters away an elderly woman reaches out.

Eugenio's disgust began to turn to something hard and cold as he continued to review the images. He hit the pause button hard enough to make an audible thunk.

An unmistakable anger seethed in him—and only with a conscious effort did he stand up and walk away from the reader, seeking some distraction. He walked to the row of windows across the room and looked out on the fountain below. Near it, a tree was being devoured by what looked to be tens of thousands of caterpillars. Eugenio turned away from the sight in revulsion.

His reactions seemed to be out of his control. Looking at the images, he hadn't become desensitized as he should have with the exposure. In fact, it seemed to have the opposite effect. Instead of fear he felt anger; even now an irrational part of him wished he saw birds at the fountain below, birds that from this distance and angle would be easy to eliminate. Eugenio stopped in mid-thought. What if this wasn't just his reaction; what if this was a common one? He'd thought before that the birds had been blamed because they were an easy culprit, a common enough vector for disease, but perhaps it had been as much revenge as lack of scientific rigor. Still—

He hurried back to the desk and picked up his tablet, linking in to the Net even before he sat down. Immediately he sought out the World Health site. The page wouldn't load. He went back in through a different network. The page stayed frozen on an error message. He'd thought the issue had been his weak network at home, but perhaps not. He tried to come in through the hardline, but still had no luck. He needed a sat link, and knew where to find the closest one. Quickly, Eugenio packed up his things and dialed up a trans to take him down-river to Meta, the closest Mendejano outpost.

❖ ❖ ❖

The October that Eugenio met Lucine the river had swelled to levels not seen since his grandparents' time. Standing on the bank nearest campus, Eugenio, fresh from a run, looked out over the river wondering how long the journey to its mouth would take. He had three weeks of fall break to conduct his research, but flooding would all but cancel his trip. He'd been checking the weather reports. All agreed that flooding was possible but not probable. With this scant comfort Eugenio boarded the fully automatic river winder his family had subsidized and checked back over his supplies, confirming that the boat was fully stocked.

He'd be interviewing residents in traditional communities along the river coast about their attitudes towards time-delayed communication and estrangement during travel to and from outlying colonies, as well as its effect on kinship groups and sense of cultural identity. He might pursue the topic for his dissertation; so this was his dry run. But just as importantly he would be in the jungle, surrounded by birds. He'd bitten his nails down to the nub at the thought and endured a bout of prelaunch hyperventilating but Eugenio had determined that the time to conquer his fear had come.

He could never be a decent medical anthropologist if the sound of birds set his teeth on edge. This was the secret goal of his trip. No one would accompany him on his cognitive therapy. He could and would fix himself and then he would go on to fix others. Eugenio broke a ceremonial bottle of rum against the bow of the ship and pressed a single blue button on his remote that gave his fate over to the boat. He stayed out on deck and looked eagerly into the distance squinting toward his certain and illustrious future.

Two days into his trip, rain fell in thick, sweeping sheets. The weather reports showed a map of where Eugenio traveled; a red cone of storm activity dominated the space. The boat tried to compensate for the rough water, but despite its efforts, Eugenio still felt the lift and lull of the water worrying his stomach. He tried to concentrate on the work before him. He sat at a small desk below deck, scribbling notes on a pad while he played back yesterday's interviews. He had visited with three households and gotten a few hours of recording. Unfortunately Eugenio seemed to have done a great deal of the talking. His questions were too long and leading; he'd quashed some opportunities to elaborate, but overall the information would be usable. On the next stop he—

The boat tilted to the extreme right and Eugenio's stomach lurched. Before he could fully recover, another wave knocked the recordings onto the floor. As Eugenio tried to stand and make his way over to the instrument console a third hit knocked him to his knees.

The ceiling alarm of the cabin flashed yellow, then quickly to orange. He crawled the meter to the console, turned on the deck lights, and looked at the monitors that showed the small deck of the ship. Caps of white water churned in the floodlights. There shouldn't be any rapids on this route. He looked over at the navigation monitor to check his location. The screen was black. Cursing, he stumbled up on deck to get an idea how far from shore he might be and how far off course the boat may have been pushed. As he reached the top of the stairs, Eugenio felt the bow of the ship slowly lift.

For a second he could see nothing but blackness, then utter stillness in front of the boat. He realized with horror it was open air. The boat hung for a second in stillness. Then, it crashed down, over a waterfall, pulling Eugenio violently forward. He cracked his forehead against the railing, and then blackness as he slammed into the water.

Sputtering and coughing, he fought to stay on the surface, pulling his body through the violent waters toward the shore.

His chest burned with the effort of closing the short distance. A strong swimmer, Eugenio felt he barely moved. His right leg was useless; the muscles in his shoulders and arms ached beyond pain. Pieces of the ship and his belongings rushed past him in the water, scraping along the length of him, and beating at his legs. Finally, he felt rocks beneath his left foot and he scrambled forward. Trying to put weight on his right foot, he nearly screamed from a flash of agony and fell into the silt. He crawled up to shore. Even before he pulled himself completely out of the water, he collapsed.

Eugenio looked down at the wreck of his knee, and wanted to cry for what he saw as much as for the searing pain that shot up through his thigh and into his groin. A patch of exposed bone was clearly visible through his shredded pant leg. Torn skin and ligament surrounded his exposed kneecap with one flap of flesh seeping a steady pulse of thick blood. Wisps of it swirled and bled into the water. Rain soaked him as he lay on his side, jaw exhausted from clenching against the pain. He had heard that people passed out in such straits, but much as Eugenio wanted that, he remained conscious, feeling the cold rain beating down on his face. Nausea came in a wave right after the misery from his knee, pinning him between pains in his stomach and those in the rest of his body as he lay gasping on the shore. He turned his head to retch and caught a glimpse of the wreck of the river winder being dragged downstream.

His food and water, recordings, and camping gear had been washed away in the storm that capsized the boat. He'd been the only thing to make it out of the boat. At that moment he felt every molecule a thing, cold and alone in the jungle, the thoughts of conquest and knowledge that had brought him so far from home gone from his mind. A woodpecker peeped out from a nearby treehole and regarded him coolly.

His misery, at least, overcame his fear of birds for the moment. He took no solace, but a grim satisfaction at that. The overwhelming din of rain beating into the water drowned out the sound of approaching footsteps. He didn't hear them until someone squelched in the mud a meter from him. Eugenio turned towards the sound and saw a striking olive-skinned woman standing nearly over him. She wore simple cotton slacks tucked into black boots and a worn slicker; a battered wide-brimmed hat sat atop her head. Rain ran along the brim of the hat she wore and dripped down onto his leg. Eugenio tried to remember how to greet someone in one of the dialects of the river bank, but his mind wouldn't work.

The woman knelt down near his leg, took a cursory look at the wound clearly visible through the shreds of his pants leg.

"Where's your GPS?" she asked just as clearly as one of his fellow students.

Eugenio peered up at her, afraid he might vomit if he opened his mouth. He took a deep breath and answered. "In the river. With everything else."

"So help won't be coming. Or at least not too soon. You won't be able to walk on that," she said, gesturing to his knee. She stood and glanced over her shoulder at the trees behind her. "We'll need a stretcher."

"You don't have a GPS?" Eugenio asked. Everyone in Leiodare had a GPS; a few even had it discreetly hardwired into them.

"I don't need one. I know where I am." She met his gaze. "I know where I'm going."

There was no contempt or irritation in her tone. She spoke with such certainty, Eugenio's head cleared for a moment.

"I'm Eugenio."

She reached into her pants pocket and pulled out a small plastic pouch. She unzipped it and removed two red pills. She held the tablets out to him.

"My name is Lucine. This will help the pain." She knelt down near his head.

Eugenio hesitated, then took the pills.

"Sick of this rain yet, Eugenio?"

He nodded miserably.

"Let's get to work on that stretcher then." Lucine hooked her hands into his armpits and drug him towards the trees, leaving a deep swath in the mud.

Under the partial cover of trees, she assembled a travois stretcher from three macheted branches. Eugenio watched as she padded it sparsely with a long, bulky shirt she removed from under her slicker. When the stretcher was complete, Eugenio rolled on and they started the trek into town.

Eugenio expected her to take him to a quaint settlement that looked like it belonged in another age. Bare-chested children would be running around a group of houses that resembled the images he'd found in the library, with thatched solar scrap roofs and round foundations. Elders would be seated on covered porches casting charms and smoking from long wooden pipes fashioned from the surrounding trees.

When she drug his stretcher the last few meters he couldn't have been more wrong. Lucine took him to a small township on the outskirts of the jungle. If it resembled anything, it was a Leiodaran neighborhood, and not one in The Dire or near The Dumps—not even Smoketown, but one of the middle-class enclaves that had a view of The Spires. The stuccoed homes were lined up along a long wide lane, paved and smooth as asphalt. At the head of the lane, a sculpture of a large circle had been constructed from light boxes.

"What's the sculpture?" Eugenio asked.

"It's a symbol. The central symbol of the Mendejano."

From this angle Eugenio hadn't been able to tell there were inner circles, but the realization that it was Mendejano excited him. Despite his pain, Eugenio's mind sparked at the idea of it.

"Is this a Mendejano village?"

Lucine stopped pulling and turned her attention to him.

"Does this look like a village?" As she finished posing the question, a stunning young woman with a jagged scar on her jaw walked past fiddling with the blacked goggles of a top-of-the-line virtu rig.

He realized he had offended her. It was the last thing he wanted to do, considering all she had already done for him and certainly no way to start an interview. Plus just gazing into her dark eyes, he felt a keen desire to please this woman and he'd done just the opposite.

"No, it reminds me of home."

"Leiodare, must be; closest city with men who are no good with boats. Yes, I've been there, but everything here is built a bit lower to the ground, no skyscrapers here. We're going there." She pointed at a large building with a veranda in front. "The doctor should be in."

The doctor did not have good news.

The damage done on the ship and the apparent drubbing as he made his way to the shore had severely damaged his knee. He would need surgery and though the doctor could perform a rudimentary fix it wouldn't compare to the care available back in the city. The doctor stabilized him and suggested that he return to Leiodare immediately. They could transport him to a heliport and have him back there that same day. Eugenio lay on the examining table staring at the soft yellow light beaming down on him. He had listened quietly and now appeared to be considering.

"Are you Mendejano?" he asked Lucine.

"I have that honor, yes," Lucine replied. "But it's not what you think—not what you've heard."

"Why don't you tell me then?" Eugenio said. Quietly he was pleased with himself.

"Do I look like a storyteller to you? Are we in the middle of some extravagant tour? A total immersion vacation?"

Eugenio's pleasure fizzled away.

"I only meant—"

"You only meant." She turned and eyed Eugenio with the same still stare she'd shown earlier. He'd offended her again and was running out of hope that he could salvage the situation. He tried not appear as tired and defeated as he felt.

After a moment she exhaled, paused briefly and began to speak. He could hear the tension drain from her voice in the first few sentences. "You and Jose are alike. He too was trapped by the whim of the water. Though in his case you could also imply it was man—those who watched the waters rise and did nothing as well as himself. Jose Mendejano lived on Isla de la Juventud. He intended to be the last man to leave it, and as the waters rose, he became the last person there. Each night he looked toward Havana in the north, and bid it and the seagulls good night. Never being sure if he would drown before morning, he prayed that the gulls would ferry his soul beyond should the need arise.

"Records have made it apparent that the danger of drowning may have been a poetic turn more than an actual possibility. But eventually the day came that he woke to water just outside his door. The water had carried his boat away and swimming to Havana one hundred kilometers north was just as possible as swimming to the moon. At that time, Jose had more passion than practicality, so only then did he realize how incomplete his plan had been. He pulled out his handheld to call for help—but just then something occurred to him.

"For one thing, if he called for help now, he'd be calling for help all his life, and for another, he had no great desire to be told he had been foolish to think he could accomplish anything more than a hollow victory by sitting and watching the island sink. He could not hold back the ocean, they would say, as they had said before. Of course this was correct; Jose was many things but none of them a fool. Holding back the ocean had never been the point. Also, he was tired of no one ever understanding the point. So he sat down and sorted out a way to get himself off that island so that he could have what he had wanted and go on to the next.

"In the sixteen months it took him to build not only a raft, but a boat, and more than that, a vessel packed with smoked fish, crab, and clothes, Jose was overcome with desire. He wanted to share what he had learned. Also, he was probably terribly lonely, but they tend to trim these bits from such tales. Anyway, he broadcast his message on a pirate satellite program and beamed it in short regular bursts. He'd originally acquired the software because he planned on sending the birth and death date of Isla de la Juventud, as suggested by an online friend. But this seemed a better use.

"By the time he sailed around the eastern edge of the island and reached Havana, Jose had begun to broadcast regularly. He started out simply: Anything can be fixed. Every object is a tool. We know what's broken and we need only find how.

"He included instruction on planing pine with a stone wedge, programming a stealth security site, and the best way to catch snook with a line—but he always came back to these central points. Anything can be fixed; every object is a tool; we know what's broken; we need only find how. Soon he began to receive messages from others. They had worked together and found him by tracing back his own satellite signal. With a powered GPS web and pinged handheld messages they could speak to him directly during his journey.

"Devising a way to overcome the distance made his listeners feel strong, empowered. They had found their guru. Here was something they could do, something they had done! In this world, where so much lay beyond their control. Prairies slowly turned to deserts, individual people began to outlive whole species, and international borders shifted. But now they had some power in the world. Anything can be fixed;

the only question was how. It was better than optimism. It was certainty.

"After spending days and nights speaking to his listeners, Jose charted a new course to Florida, the southernmost tip. There, in Naples, he found people waiting for him on the shore. When he arrived they took him to a bungalow they'd rented for the occasion and told stories of what they had fixed while he was en route. Some of the people stayed there and began a commune that became the first settlement. They started to call themselves Mendejano because Jose had told them on his arrival, 'Bienvenidos, familia. It's wonderful to be home.'

"Jose sailed around the world in that dugout canoe. It took him a decade, and in those years he stopped countless times along the way, teaching and learning, but mostly visiting with us all."

Eugenio lay on the cot, more interested in Lucine's tale than he'd anticipated. Professional curiosity aside, Jose Mendejano's story stuck with him for the rest of the afternoon. When the medivac came, he refused to leave. He asked the doctor if she would tell him how to fix the torn ligaments in his knee.

"With surgery in Leiodare," she answered, exasperated.

After several hours of talking and two missed cycles of painkillers, he still hadn't convinced Lucine or the doctor he shouldn't immediately go back to Leiodare for surgery.

"Definitely crazy. Perhaps brave, but certainly stupid, Eugenio. You should go now and have the surgery," Lucine said.

"Will you help me, if I have the surgery?" he asked.

"Help you with what?"

"To fix myself."

"And what will do that?"

"Becoming Mendejano."

Lucine turned to him, bemused, but perhaps, Eugenio thought, with a glimmer of respect.

Even after the surgery, his knee had never been quite right, but Eugenio had his compensations.

He and Lucine became twins just before Eugenio's thirty-third birthday. He'd graduated with his PhD/MSc and made his way down the river in a dugout canoe he'd built with his two hands and a chainsaw. Lucine laughed at him, making fun of his literal nature, and they loaded up her truck for the trip back into the city, she on her mission and he on his.

Eugenio hadn't been back since that day, but he found Meta largely unchanged. He hopped out of the trans, and looking warily up for birds, hurried to Kizzy's doctor office. When he slammed the door shut behind him, out of breath, she shook her head and smiled at him.

"Oh, Eugenio, always such a dramatic entrance," Kizzy said.

"I do my best. Is your sat link up?"

"Yes, I was just logging off—finished a seminar," she answered.

"Don't bother. If it's all right with you I'd like to use it for some research."

"More on the Crumble, I expect," Kizzy said.

"Yes," he replied.

She stood up. "It's all yours," she said.

"Thank you, Kizzy."

"Good luck." She squeezed his shoulder. "It's good to see you. Next time, bring your sister!"

Eugenio got to work. Though it took a few hours of searching primary and secondary files he found it, on an obscure subdrive and directory he'd stumbled on almost by accident. The subdrive included a list of personal effects recovered from Peter Warrel's hotel room. The fifth item on the list caught Eugenio's attention: an ID badge from the conference Peter Warrel had been in town attending. The badge listed his name—under a trademarked

icon that Eugenio had seen for years around town, and most recently stamped into the pavers of McClaren Street.

Eugenio took a screen shot of the file and sent it to his boss, as well as the head of the Emergency Management Division, and the one person associated with McClaren Industries who might be more invested in the truth than the company's image.

They'd all be interested to know that Patient Zero had been attending a McClaren Industries conference; it couldn't be a coincidence. Rory McClaren had been wrong. It wasn't all done, not at all.

10

Rory lit a candle for Katherine's birthday, as was his custom. He stood in the flickering shadows with the shades drawn, staring at the flame as images of his sister and the rest of his family floated past on holo. He tried to absorb the three-dimensional slideshow with which he always celebrated her birthday, but it seemed even more hollow than it had last year and the year before. Over the years, Rory had found thousands of images of his family online and downloaded dozens of them, but they were press images: PR photo ops with rehearsed smiles and product placements. They made him feel much the same way he expected they must make any other stranger feel: *my, what nice looking people, they look very well-to-do, wonder what they're hiding.*

In his mother's photos one could tell. She had a gift for capturing not just a certain expression of personal reverie, but choosing the perfect one. He had once watched her review over two hundred photos in an afternoon to find one of his Pop Pop that she thought showed him clearly: his funeral photo. They had given him his Last Word, but his mother had wanted the photo to sit on the easel next to the sleek metal case that contained his ashes. In the photo, Pop Pop held the black lab puppy his sister had bought for his eighty-second birthday. Pop Pop and the dog had matching hair and the same laughing eyes. For this reason, he had named the dog Jack, short for jackass.

Over the years, Rory'd thought of the photos thousands of times. Sometimes they seemed the only proof that Katherine, Mom, and the girls hadn't been some elaborate hallucination designed to whittle his mind into a sharp stick that he would one day fall upon. At times, it seemed to him that only his mother's photos would save him from that fate. But he didn't want a stranger rifling through his family's things.

Rory had tried to go home once before, on the fifth day after he locked himself inside the apartment so many years ago. Standing at the door with his hands shoved into his jacket pockets, nowhere near the palmlock, he cursed himself.

"Ridiculous. You're a grown goddamned man! A goddamn soldier!" he screamed red-faced at the door. He'd been standing there for fifteen minutes with visions of his family playing through his head. His repeated calls still hadn't brought a response. The service wouldn't take any more messages. The circuits were overwhelmed.

Rory wanted to think that they'd evacuated already or maybe that the phone in the panic wing had been disconnected for some reason. His contacts outside the city hadn't heard from his family either. So he stood there unsuccessfully willing himself forward.

He'd never known such fear and he couldn't understand it. His hand shook each time he reached out for the palmlock, and much as Rory didn't want to admit it, the thought of going outside made him nauseous. What would he do if he came across an infected person? Hell, when he came upon an infected person? The holo reports had already brought phantasms of former people, now walking corpses, whose faces had begun to cave in. Their pitiful wails could be heard faintly in the wind, and from the reports. He kept muting the reports, then turning the sound back up when a faint cry reached him from the street. Rory tried changing the channel, but couldn't stand not knowing what went on beyond the front door.

Disgusted, he'd gotten dressed and packed a bag for the journey. No trans service would come pick him up, and per the reports the trains weren't running. If he wanted to get to McClaren Street, he would have to walk.

There were reported suspicions that the virus was airborne. That couldn't matter now. He had to see how they were. But the reports said it killed quickly and it had been five days. He stopped the thought, and his right hand lurched out once more and input the first two numbers into the pad, then Rory pulled his hand back as if it had been burned. Tears of frustration welled up in his eyes.

"God. Damn. It!"

In the silence that followed, the sound of muted pleading reached him through the door. It must have been from the street, but it sounded so close, too close. Rory backed slowly away from it, his gaze locked on the barrier that separated him from infection. His handheld rang loudly and he jumped, wrestling it out of his pocket. Katherine's image appeared on the display. "Katherine!" He punched the talk button. "Katherine?"

"It's me," she replied quietly.

"Thank God." He shook with relief.

"Mom's gone. The girls are gone, Rory," Katherine whispered. "Wherever you are, you stay there," she said. "Don't you come out in this."

"Gone? What do you mean they're gone? Katherine, please. How? It's only been a few days."

"I have to go now."

"What?! No, Katherine. Tell me. Where are you now? Talk to me," Rory pleaded.

"I love you, Roar," she said. And she was gone.

Katherine didn't die by disease. When her suicide had been confirmed, Rory did what his sister had told him to. He did not go out; instead he had ordered the family house closed. He gave strict orders that the family place be decontaminated, cleaned, and sealed. ICDC would not release the bodies to him. The McClaren women shared the same cremation as everyone who perished that winter, a single ceremony on March twenty-seventh—attended by few but watched by hundreds of millions via video feed.

And on top of all that, someone half-crazy with grief at city administration had decided they should play the confessionals. The booths had been erected as a local McClaren Industries research and development evaluation. Research and development frequently used Leiodare and Leiodarans as the backdrop and subjects for its latest innovations and potential product lines. With McClaren Industries and research and development headquartered in Leiodare it made sense to test them on its diverse, transient population. And in a world obsessed with commemorating its own life, the idea of satellite booths where a patron could record their own thoughts, feelings, and spectral image for archives and broadcast seemed a good one. No one at McClaren had planned on the name of "confessionals"; they were much more enamored with their own Studio™. The booths could be found on streets in The Shallows and near The Spires, as common as telephone booths had been once, Pop Pop said.

No one had any idea what role the messages recorded in these booths would play in the Crumble, but that role had of course become as well known as the Crumble itself, and synonymous with Leiodare. For years, The Last Word had been too expensive for most people to use, but the booths changed all that. They had specifically been placed in The Shallows to see what range of demographics chose to use the booths. Predictably, drunk people loved them and more than once the research and development recon team collected the data discs left inside and loaded in their communications trans only to find reals that would make a porn star blush, and a doctor woozy. But more interesting than these were the unexpected visits from shopkeepers and children (a veritable untapped market) who spoke about their wrongs, their fears, their lives in a raw confession few of them would probably share with anyone face to face. Little did they know that their most private moments would be broadcast and re-broadcast around the world.

Rory did not watch the ceremony held for the city and he did not watch the confessionals. He made arrangements for the family estate and the other extensive real estate holdings on McClaren Street, placing them in trust, and waited to feel differently. For the last twenty-five years a remote tech ran systems for half a day every three months, and no more, no cleaning crew, no journalists or historians, no visitors.

Everything that had been in the house during that winter remained. His mother's photographs, handsomely framed black-and-white images from their childhoods and from her own, still decorated the walls of the house. One of Katherine's sweaters, no doubt, still hung somewhere on the back of a chair. His nieces' drawings still covered the refrigerator in the back kitchen. Rory stared into the candlelight, envisioning those details. The thought of this permanency comforted him, as much now as when he'd made the arrangements in the cramped apartment where he had dreaded their demise. One thing in particular he thought of often.

He wanted those photos. The images only existed in one place, his mother's personal collection. Seeing them would be like looking through her eyes, her perspective on the intimate moments that made them family.

He knew one person who wasn't a stranger, one person who might be able to do what he could not. Watching the wax weep from the wick, Rory contemplated placing the call.

He had been saving Peru for a rainy day. He'd commissioned reals from any number of stars in the field. For every kind of real there was a different class of virtuoso who excelled at it—a mainliner who specialized in extreme stunts and face-offs would be useless if the client wanted an intimate encounter with a favorite starlet. He'd linked into Peru's work before and been impressed—not with the neuro peaks or courage, but more so with her blasé calm. In that way she seemed like the Rory of Yore that he had begun to crave the way he had once craved a new lover, a new frontier, a new real. And so he had begun to crave Peru.

He'd started his bidding modestly. Peru was good but became less attractive to the general market with each passing year. Her emotional readings slunk down over time. Though lots of virtuosos got too used to their work, Peru's peaks had once been so high that the drop showed clearly.

Rory had gotten hold of some of her classic work: a whitewater trip that ended with an impromptu mud slide—an unbelievable ride, and one she handled calmly. But, people wanted to feel exhilarated when they drove two hundred kilometers per hour down a twisting country road, not as if they were reading the paper at a corner café. Not even if that was because reading at the corner café felt as exhilarating as that breakneck boat ride.

Peru's steady readings meant she might be suitable for psych projects, but judging from her reals Rory didn't think she had the disposition to deal with the administrative side of those kind of assignments. So though he wanted her work badly, chances were, Rory was probably part of a shrinking pool of potential commission clients. So the businessman in him offered less than half of what he would pay.

Starting where he did, she refused the first several offers. In fact Peru didn't even bother to have her agent respond. Most virtuosos, in fact, most people, wouldn't try this with a McClaren. The money behind the name usually did all of Rory's work; once he'd been vetted to be who he purported to be, his agent might be able to get the Pope to record a real for Rory. So Peru's reticence earned some respect and he redoubled his efforts, but not his bids.

Over time, his agent sent word to hers less and less often, but always offered more. It proved to be a winning strategy.

He convinced her with a sum of money and a promise of more to come. As it turned out Peru didn't want one big score; she wanted a steady income. So in the summer of that year Peru had moved to Leiodare and Rory, for the first time in many years, took a visitor. He had very much wanted to meet this woman who would become his eyes and ears to the world outside. For the kind of work he wanted done, he had to be sure Peru was who he believed her to be. Rory had paid for a first-class ticket and escort to bring her to him, or as close as anyone ever came—the anteroom just outside the elevator into his rooms. Peru had refused the escort and taken the train into the city. She did, however, come directly to The Spires upon her arrival.

She stood in the anteroom with her hands folded in front of her as if presenting herself for the service. Rory sat in his great room sipping a gewürztraminer in the shadows. Three layers of shatterproof plexi separated them.

Peru's appearance was different than he would have guessed. On a real, a competent virtuoso never looked in a reflective surface or otherwise showed his or her face unless the client directly requested a reveal. Rory never made such requests. So he sat, taking her in for the first time. His first thought was that Peru didn't appear the least bit Peruvian. Though she had black hair and brown eyes, something in the structure of her face didn't remind him of that place. In fact, she reminded Rory a bit of himself. Virtuosos seemed to choose their names purely for marketing purposes, but one did run into those who had named themselves after an ancestral home. But seeing her now, Peru didn't seem to fit into that category. Rory studied her precariously high cheekbones, and short jagged scar at the corner of her jaw, the dead-set dazzle of her gaze and felt more intrigued by this woman.

"Where will you stay?" he asked.

"Why do you care?" Peru responded.

"Because it will show in the real. Whether you like the place or are getting enough rest, whether the food is agreeing with you. Everything shows up in the real. And I'm paying for it. I want you as you are. As you've been. Too much change will affect that."

"Then why did you bring me here? That's change," she said.

Rory peered at Peru, considering. She didn't seem to care enough to be cautious of how she spoke to him. Perhaps what he took for calm was just self-destruction. Or sharp apathy. Still, he could use that. Or perhaps he'd become too accustomed to those who did his bidding without question or concern. Challenge was new.

"This is where it happened," Rory replied. "So what has to be done, has to be done here."

"What is to be done?" Peru asked.

Rory stood and walked over into the light, until he was just a few meters from the plexi.

"You're going to do something I've wanted to for twenty-five years."

And of course, she hadn't. He'd assigned Peru dozens of reals in the last three years. But not yet this one. Rory had postponed it countless times, sending her off to explore some new part of town first. But now he would finally ask her to go to the family home and to make a real of it.

He'd even dreamed of it: the ring of absolute silence that always followed pressing the virtu rig's 'Play' button. And then in it would flood, the real's world. He'd waited so long for this particular real, the one he'd searched through dozens of virtuosos for, who felt purely and powerfully enough to approximate the feelings he would have felt if he could have done it himself. Rory had found her, and wooed her and honed her. Now he needed to send her on the assignment that would mean more than all the others, to be his proxy and bring him home and his family back.

"Call—" Rory began.

"One new message," the home system interrupted.

"Ignore," Rory said with irritation. "Call Peru."

The line rang a dozen times before an automated voice prompted him to leave a message.

"Call me immediately. I have an assignment," Rory said. His annoyance grew. This was the second time he'd called Peru to be greeted by her answering service. He hadn't heard from or spoken to her in days—for the amount he paid her as a retainer fee, this should never happen. He started to dial his security to track her down when he remembered the new message. Perhaps she'd been in touch after all.

"Play message."

A man's voice began to speak.

"Mr. McClaren. This is Dr. Oliveira, Eugenio Oliveira. Mr. McClaren, I've found something I think you should know about. It's not all done as you said. Peter Warrel, that engineer, you know the one, he was attending a McClaren Industries conference. That's all I could find in the public records. There are no other records that I have access to. But I imagine you are a man with many more resources than I. I hope to speak with you soon."

Rory collapsed on the divan. The holos continued to drift past him as his thoughts raced. How could he have not known that? Rory shook his head. Of course, he wouldn't have known that. He attended the quarterly meetings he was required to and usually messaged his friends and conquests throughout. One thing he did know though was that every McClaren conference was a preamble or pretext to research and development. And if Warrell had been at the conference there had to be a connection between his work and McClaren—and quite possibly one between that work and the Crumble. That kind of outbreak and infection had never been seen before. Research

& Development existed to create what had never been seen before. What had they developed that year?

"Log in to remote access McClaren Industries intranet. Prepare for retinal scan." Rory pushed himself up and walked over to the scanner, placing his eye in its beam.

"Access granted."

"Search research and development. Keyword—"

"Access denied. Research and development modules are not accessible by remote server."

Rory clenched his jaw and stared into nothingness, trying to figure out a solution.

"Log off."

There had to be some way of accessing those files. He had to know if there was a connection. He tried to remember the names of any trusted contacts or malleable flunkies who might still be available. He had to get to those files. He stopped on the brink of the next thought. Those files. Maybe not those, but his own. Twenty-five-year-old files were about the only drives he had at the penthouse.

Rory turned in one fluid motion and strode toward the library.

11

The second time that Anna met Seife she had an unmistakable reaction to the feel of Seife's skin beneath her hand. Anna had seen Seife as soon as she entered the station. She approached the other woman from behind and laid her hand momentarily on Seife's shoulder to get her attention. At first contact, a single, impolite, and powerful throb made it difficult for Anna to meet Seife's eyes. When it subsided, they still stood in the train station inside a burgundy beam of light waiting for the train that would take them separate ways. Anna mustered up her courage.

"Hello," Anna said. Not terribly original, she thought.

"Hello," Seife answered, a broad smile blooming on her face."I have your parcels."

Anna's eyebrows knitted together. "My parcels. . ."

"The ones you left at the club," Seife said.

"You kept them for me?"

"And this surprises you?" Seife replied, a hint of playfulness in her tone.

"Yes, it does."

"Well, I have them. I mean, they are at the club, safe. No need to worry, Anna Armour."

"Please, just call me Anna."

"You said . . ."

"It sounds so formal when you say it. Just Anna." She smiled.

"Anna," Seife said it softly, as much a whisper as a word.

Warmth rushed to Anna's face. "So what brings you to McClaren? So late in the day I mean. You seem to have some parcels of your own." Anna pointed at the bag Seife held.

"Yes, it's an old format piece I've wanted. A special recording."

"There's a song I've been thinking about these past few days—"

"The Life of Ever," Seife finished.

Anna looked over at her slyly.

"Do you know it?" Seife continued.

"You know I do."

"Yes, I suppose I do," Seife said; she looked at Anna intently. "Have dinner with me—before all."

Anna laughed, pushed an errant tendril of hair behind her ear. "Where shall we go?"

"Smoketown, the best food in the city."

They rode the train as far as The Dire and came topside so that Seife could give Anna a walking tour. Night had started to fall. As the last indigo of sunset settled into the shadows, they turned off the smooth sidewalk and ventured onto a path created by footsteps and not much else. Within a few meters, just outside The Dire, the trees began. Insects chirped and swooped around them, a soft blanket of sound that surrounded them. Small glow globes illuminated the increasing darkness. Tree trunks and foliage sprouted as far back as Anna could see, clearly demarcating their departure from the most urban areas of Leiodare. It felt ten degrees cooler in the trees. One hundred and fifty meters in, a line of earthen mounds stood three meters high; smoke rose steadily from them.

"What are they?" Anna asked.

"The kilns."

"The bones," Anna said.

"Yes, bone black. We burn the bones in these kilns, some ceramics in a larger one further in. Most people don't know that name, bone black," Seife said, sounding impressed.

"That's probably because drawing charcoal is rarely made from bones these days." A soft breeze blew across Anna's forehead and oddly she wondered if she could draw a breeze into existence.

"Are you an artist?" Seife asked, turning to Anna.

"Of sorts," Anna answered.

"Smoketown has a lot of bones available. We abut the fence. Most of the charcoal, we ship out as biochar. The other city-states bury it to offset global warming. And we keep a bit for local artists. But I haven't seen you at any of the art markets."

"No, I've never been. Just came across some at work." Discussing the subject of her art made Anna slightly uncomfortable. To change the subject, she said the first thing that came to mind. "Why did you talk to me at the club?"

Perhaps she should have said the second thing, she thought.

"You seemed different than the people who usually follow me."

Anna started to chuckle, but Seife's expression stopped her. "People follow you?"

"I've been identified before, so yes. All the callers have. I used to live outside Smoketown, but it was too dangerous. I had a flat near the Gardens—small, but quite lovely. Big windows and all these antique details that gave it character—tray ceilings and solar thermal collectors, all that. But I couldn't stay because some guy had found out who I was and where I lived, and then another. My first two years calling I had to move three times, get rid of seven handhelds and stab a man."

"And yet you talked to me?"

Seife made a noncommittal noise and shrugged her shoulders.

"No, you talked to me. You talked to me like I was a person, no awe or lust. Not even weird curiosity. That's beyond rare. Even when I leave the city, if people find out it's the same. You don't act like that. You even left in the middle of one of my shows," she finished, a mock expression of offense on her face.

"I apologize for that," Anna said, feeling sheepish.

"Apology accepted. You can make it up to me by taking me to dinner," Seife said playfully.

Shortly, Anna and Seife rounded a hill on their path. Smoketown's homes came into view. They were built far above the ground, some halfway to the treetops, others further still. Most had been constructed of wood. They looked like large redwood-colored cubes that stood in the treetops, upwind from the kilns. Each house was stained a warm reddish brown and had long, narrow windows, the height of three planks that ran around the perimeter, more bands of glass than traditional windows. The number of windows and their placement in the houses differed. Many homes had a window that crossed the corner of the house so that it took up half of two walls. A few had the windows across every corner and wall, so that the band of glass encircled the entire home. Two long tree trunks connected to a metal platform supported the houses. Staircases—spiral, straight or staggered—led up to them.

"Is this the way people used to live here?" Anna asked.

"No, people used to live on the ground here. It was once the largest Black neighborhood in the old city, and they made bricks here so they lived in squat, solid houses a tornado couldn't touch. My great-uncle used to have printouts from photos—actual photos—in black and white. It looked like another planet, but the faces were the same." She joined Anna's laughter.

"Now we build in the trees because of the beetles. If they ever came this far east, they'd roll out into the jungle without disrupting anything. We find that the bugs are only unavoidable if you don't adapt."

"Where's your place?" Anna asked.

"Back beyond that band of trees, closer to the perimeter." She then pointed farther east. "Right now we're going there."

"There" resembled one of the old water towers that Anna had grown up seeing, a short, fat cylinder with a pointed roof. But where those water towers had been rusted-out remnants of another age, this one had smooth white walls and glittering firefly lights that surrounded the windows. Like Smoketown's other buildings, it stood high in the trees atop a platform. Anna followed Seife up the stairs, led there by the delicious aroma as much as the woman in front of her.

According to the menu, the restaurant Desta served African fusion food with a "Smoketown flair."

Inside, an intoxicating mixture of spice and sweetness filled the air in the small space, fueled by the bouquet of foreign spices and heaping portions of delicious, slow-cooked food. Seife and Anna sat on a pair of low stools near the picture window. A waitress came, and after taking their orders, placed a huge circle of injera bread between them. Mounds of doro wat, ackee, and spiced cabbage, among others lined the edges of the bread. The restaurant offered both resin and honey wines. A glass of each sparkled on small tables next to the larger table; additional fluffy triangles of folded injera also shared that space. Seife returned from washing her hands. She watched as Anna toweled her hands dry, preparing to delve into their meal. Anna ripped a large triangle in half, grabbed some of the spicy chicken with it and placed it in her mouth. Pleasure flooded through her.

"You like the doro wat?" Seife asked.

"Mmmm," Anna responded.

Seife laughed and sipped her wine. "You know Ethiopian food then?"

"Yes, I enjoy it very much." Anna smelled the rich scent of teff on her breath as she spoke.

"This is the only restaurant that serves Ethiopian in Leiodare. Yet I have never seen you here."

"That's because I've never been. I had it before," Anna said.

"So you are not from the city?" Seife asked.

"You know that." Anna knew as well as Seife that she was an obvious outsider.

"I do." She returned Anna's gaze. "How do you know I know?"

"Because you are from here."

"How—" Seife began.

"Aren't all callers from Leiodare?" Anna asked.

"Most are from Smoketown. A few from Leiodare." Seife brought a bite of food up to her mouth.

"Smoketown is in Leiodare. What's the distinction?"

"Smoketown is *of* Leiodare."

Anna waited for Seife to explain, filling the silence and her mouth with another helping of chicken and this time with a bit of cabbage to couple with the spice.

"There's more than a few kilometers between the two," Seife said. "But I suppose you are right. Smoketown is part of Leiodare, but it is very different."

"Like The Dire from The Spires?" Anna teased.

Seife looked at Anna slowly so that her own lack of amusement spread across her entire expression. "Yes, I suppose you could say that. If you must."

Anna almost choked on her food. "A good deadpan—that's difficult to come by in these parts."

"Nearly as difficult as a witty dinner companion, I expect," Seife said.

Anna laughed openly. The sound plainly startled Seife. Seife could not know, but the sound of Anna's own high, mischievous laughter surprised Anna as well.

"So when did you start singing? Did you take lessons?" Anna asked.

"Oh, you wanna hear the recitation?" Seife said sarcastically.

"Excuse me?" Anna said.

Seife took a sip of wine and cleared her throat. Anna, confused, watched as Seife sat up straight in her seat and began.

"I learned to sing by listening to my grandfather as he tended the kilns. While he loaded the sun-bleached bones into the oven, he sang a mournful song of thankfulness. Some days he would interlace his dirge with bawdy ballads. He had learned them while worked in the canopy, climbing to the treetops where he harvested trumpet blossoms for Dex Pharma."

Anna wasn't sure how to respond.

Seife laughed. "That's what I what I tell the visiting dignitaries when I'm being 'colorful'."

Anna relaxed and smiled. "You do?"

"Yes. I play the part of a quaint and intriguing exotic. I do it at all the official dinners. They're mandatory for callers."

"The exotic?" Anna made a sound of disapproval.

"True, but with most everyone some shade of brown or beige, someone has to play the part," Seife said sardonically.

"Do they?" Anna searched out Seife's gaze with her own and held it.

"Perhaps not," Seife said quietly. She touched Anna's hand briefly before she continued. "Honestly. . . well, honestly, I never learned to sing; I had to learn not to sing. Not to sing during class, at meals, while waiting for the train. That restraint was my initiation into propriety."

Anna regarded her warmly. "And look what you've done with it."

Seife laughed, spitting a morsel of food out in the process. It struck Anna's shoulder.

"Look what you've done with it," Anna repeated grimly.

When they parted, Seife had just enough time to get home and prepare for the morning's call. They stepped into the train station, the smell of oncoming rain following them underground.

"It will be a quiet call this morning. It would be nice just to laze in bed."

"I guess you can't just tell them you can't make it?" Anna said.

"Not without proper notice or a damn good reason and city transport will soon be there waiting for me, as well as security."

"You have security?" Anna asked.

"You must have seen them following us when we do the morning calls."

"No, I haven't."

"You must be more observant, Anna. The things that you must miss."

"There are things I would miss were I to look away," Anna said.

Seife's gaze softened and fell.

"You're sure you wouldn't rather I call a service? You'd be home in half the time," Seife said.

"I enjoy riding the train," Anna replied.

"I think I can understand why—" Seife began. Wind from the arriving train pushed into the station, and muffled her words.

"What's that?" Anna asked.

Seife stepped closer to Anna, so that her body was a breath away. Gently, she cupped Anna's jaw in her hand. She brought her lips to Anna's ear and said, surely it must have been softly, but for that moment Anna could hear nothing else: "More time to savor."

Seife backed away, turned and walked to the stairs.

At home, Anna bounded up the stairs two at a time. She reached her landing, feeling even more energetic than when she'd hit the building entrance. Tomorrow, she'd—

A shipping box with green stars sat outside Anna's front door. Even from this distance she knew the gray spot near the corner spelled out her initials.

Staring, she tried to collect herself, but she'd been scattered at first sight of it, all the excitement she'd felt seconds ago was swept away into a place now locked to her. Her footsteps echoed in the hallway as she walked to her door, bent, and lifted the box. Anna closed the door behind her and stood inside, staring down at the package. Slowly, she placed it on the kitchen counter. It had not been returned to sender or shipped back because of insufficient postage. There were no such stamps visible. There sat the same box with one significant change: a small digicom code had been imprinted on the top, the same kind used for the city's official business.

Anna picked the box up and took it over to her console. For a few anxious seconds she couldn't decide whether to sit or stand as she tilted the box's code for her scanner to read. She stood and waited while the welcome booted up.

It is with regret that we inform you of the expiration of Peru Alton on March 23 of this year. Peru Alton passed in an recreational accident.

The posted mark on the code was 476924—the city of Leiodare.

The room started to crowd in on Anna. She'd thought about Peru having died before, had certainly considered the possibility, but to have done so in Leiodare, while she was here, was just . . . Anna ran to the giene spa and threw up her dinner. The cygnets watched her curiously from the tub.

Now Anna was here, in this city, no longer waiting, and Peru was gone beyo—. The thought stuck. There it was: Peru's belief. Anna had heard it before: For the Mendejano, a soul without a bird to carry it beyond was doomed to walk the streets of its regrets. Anna remembered vividly Peru's connection to—her reverence for her faith. It was nothing that Anna believed, that Bly had ever believed, something completely Peru's own. Completely of herself. But Peru was not beyond. She had been here in Leiodare when she died. Anna cringed at the implication: And so Peru still was here, walking the streets of her regrets.

Unable to stand, Anna sat down on the floor, resting her head on her knees. Flashes of their mountain mornings, quiet moments after dinner when they listened to the sounds of the jungle, Peru's birthday, their trip to the clearing. The memories accumulated into resolve. The only thing worse than creating Peru was to lose her, and the only thing worse than that was leaving her lost.

Anna stood and retrieved the charcoal from her bedroom. *If enough of them are made, they'll survive.* She hoped her mother was right, and the Dire peddler as well. Either way Anna would do what she could. As she closed the apartment door behind her, she headed up to the roof.

The tower of Anna's building rose three stories into the air. It stood at the corner of the brownstone, homage to the founder's penchant for twenty-first-century Revival architecture and nostalgia for the old northeastern cities. As soon as Anna stepped out on the roof, the back of the tower stood in front of her, open and big as the feeling inside her. Thunder rolled somewhere off to the east. Anna walked to the tower and began to draw on it.

The first black bird was ornate, detailed, as she spent the brunt of her grief on its creation. Her intensity focused on small movements of her hand. Thoughts lurked below her concentration—bursting forth in flashes of sentences. Foreign words that she and Peru had learned together, virtus that they had completed, other people's dreams and nightmares upon which they'd spent their youth and bankrolled their adventures bubbled up from her despair and popped behind her eyes in brilliant flashes of color, as if she had a migraine unrivaled by any in her past. The charcoal ground against the brick, pieces of it falling to the ground as she worked.

The other birds came quickly, frantically, as she moved around the curve of the tower, one arm nearly independent in its movement while the rest of her stood stock-still. On the last bird her hand cramped. She dropped the charcoal and retreated several steps back from her work.

"Come on. Come on, goddamnit."

Anna felt certain that she saw the first drop of rain fall from the sky. The first drop didn't touch the drawings, nor did the first few. Coy, they caressed the air in front of them, moistened the asphalt beneath them, ran along the cracks and pooled at Anna's shoes. The first drop that hit a drawing streaked down one raven wing, momentarily soaked into the charcoal's black, seemed to be absorbed until—the tip of that wing bubbled out, and pushed into the night, the rain now falling on feathers with depth and movement that set Anna's teeth on edge. The wing peeled away from the brick and flapping, flailing, the black bird fell out of the wall and into the world.

Anna stepped back.

Even on the darkened rooftop she could see its keen gaze fall upon her as it hopped closer, stretched its wings and flew to the space next to her. It peered up, its glassy eyes drinking in the darkness.

Together, Anna and the bird watched as the other birds emerged, gracelessly, silently, from the wall, black birds large and small, each as perfectly formed as the last. Anna's flock glistened in the night, reflecting the moon and the city lights. They hopped around the roof, heads jerking in tiny precise movements.

She didn't know why she had expected them to be as quiet as the swans, but they weren't. Within the first moment of their emergence, they began to caw and whistle. First one and then many. Panic rose up in Anna and was immediately overtaken by resignation. These were no baby birds in need of her mothering. This flock could sound and fly and escape all without her permission or her help.

But that was why she had brought them into existence here, on this rooftop, wasn't it? She would stand and watch as they took to the sky and led Peru's soul away. Anna had the strength to stand that, at least.

Her neighbors would call the battalions soon, perhaps some would even have the courage to come up to the roof. She would stay here with the birds and wait. No sense running. No sense hiding.

The black birds appeared to care nothing for her plans. One by one they began to hop up on the edge of the roof, peering in all angles, hopping around the perimeter of the building. Anna was sure they could be seen from the street. Even in this dark night, the moon would soon reappear from behind the clouds and carve the birds' image into people's minds. As if on cue, the birds began to depart. They took to the sky and moved as one. They flew as if swimming, each downward stroke powerful enough to push them further and higher. Anna watched intently, as if she had never seen birds fly before, and for the moment it seemed that she hadn't because she couldn't recall such efficient wonder, not in her time as a virtuoso, not in her mother's care nor in Peru's. It was different than when she'd seen the cygnets even, this time the birds carried a weight away from her.

The flock of birds broke open and began, each one, to go their own direction.

No sense staying put anymore, she realized, and slowly made her way back down the stairs.

An hour later no one had kicked down the door. Not two hours later or even three. Not even a siren. Anna fell asleep in her clothes, with the cygnets lying near her feet.

12

They would have to listen to him now.

Eugenio walked with purpose to the EM head's office. He opened the door, and his mood instantly deflated. His boss, Lena, and the head of Emergency Management turned his direction as he entered, their expressions already sour.

"Oliveira," Director Vaughn, head of EM, said curtly. He was a splotchy man whose face had begun the long slide down into his neck.

"Director Vaughn," Eugenio replied, then nodded at Lena.

"Eugenio." She returned his nod. "Please, take a seat."

"You received the files?" Eugenio asked.

"Yes, indeed we did," Director Vaughn replied.

"Excellent, then I can skip the preliminary—"

"Yes, you can skip it all. I'm at a loss as to why you not only have you neglected your actual duties, but found it acceptable, and I can only assume necessary, to bring your negligence to our attention. And with an Urgent message code, no less."

Eugenio was momentarily dumbfounded.

"Sir, this was the worst public health issue in the city's history, and the first superbug of modern times."

"'Was', Oliveira, 'was'. I was head of EM during that time and I can assure you, Oliveira, the epidemic is over. There is no need to bring us into the office this late in the evening to review history. Meanwhile the citizens of this city are besieged by insect infestations and their attendant diseases, but this *relevant* public health issue is of apparently no interest to you, as you've missed the filing deadline for your last two reports."

"No, I haven't."

"They were due today, Oliveira," the director said.

"Sir, I'm a medical anthropologist, not an entomologist."

"So now you take issue with the nature of your assignments? Let me explain something to you, Oliveira: this city does not have funds to bankroll the pet projects and extensions on your dissertation topic—"

"But, sir, that dissertation was one of the reasons I was hired."

"By Dr. Stephens," Director Vaughn said, looking at her askance. "As she took it, apparently incorrectly, to be a sign of your commitment to this city's well-being. You, however, seem to be much more interested in solving non-existent mysteries and wasting the taxpayer's money. I'm putting you on sus—"

"But, sir, this is a public health issue. If nothing else, it is a mental health issue. The prevalence of ornithophobia and—"

A dark spot moved across the window behind the director's head, catching Eugenio's attention.

"I am placing you on suspension effective immediately—"

"But, sir—"

"Immediately, Oliveira."

"Who'll be handling the Crumble report while I'm on leave? I'm sure I'll have input and—"

"The Crumble report was written twenty-five years ago, Oliveira, and at this rate, it may not be a suspension. We'll re-evaluate your status in two weeks. There are some things you'll need to show us if you'd like to retain your position. The first is an approved psych evaluation stating. . ." the director said, pointing to a bullet-pointed letter on his desk.

Outside the window, the dark spot slowly shifted, changing direction back toward Emergency Management. The back of Eugenio's neck began to tingle. He leaned forward, trying to discern what he saw there in the dark.

The director balked.

"Oliveira! I'm afraid your judgment is more compromised than even I'd believed. Are you even listening to me?"

"Eugenio," Lena began. "We can get this fixed, but it has to start now, knowing and meeting these expectations will be essential to—"

Eugenio couldn't even pretend to listen to her. He hurried around the desk and the director pushed his chair back quickly to clear his path.

"What do you think you're doing?!"

Eugenio went to the window and squinted. The dark spot moved into the streetlights' beam: birds, a huge flock of birds. A small sound of shock escaped him. The director and Lena turned their gazes to the window. He spared a glance at the director. Eugenio might wear the same expression if he'd been slapped.

"Dear God," the director said. "Are those holos? Mechanicals?"

"Sir, we should adjourn," Lena said. "Those are bio."

"Adjourned," Director Vaughn agreed quietly.

Eugenio was the first out the door. Outside, he jerked his head up, irrationally expecting to see the birds diving towards him. The air here was clear, but he hurried to the aboveground train station across the street. There, a conductor waiting for his shift to begin slowly shifted his weight from foot to foot as he smoked a short thick cigar. As Eugenio watched, a sharp strange cascade of sound erupted behind the man. The conductor snatched his head around. Looking up, he peered into the manicured trees that stood at this corner with his gaze.

Uneasiness flooded through Eugenio as he watched, moving toward that end of the platform; the hair on his forearms stood away from the skin. The sound came again. The conductor took a step back, nearing the edge of the platform. Eugenio called out to him.

"Hey! Come away from there! It's—"

Something heavy fluttered in the air, sending the sound rippling out to Eugenio.

The sudden shape of a bird emerged from the blackness in front of the conductor. He flailed his arms up to shield his face. He stumbled and his body wheeled onto the tracks. Eugenio ran forward. He found the man, lying on his side, staring up into the dark, an expression of terror on his face. The sound of an incoming train filled the station. Eugenio turned to the nearest pole and hit the emergency button.

Just down the line, a commuter car ground to a halt, sending golden sparks arcing past the windows. The rail screeched. Eugenio watched helplessly as the force of the stop pushed people across the floor where they met metal and plastene and all manner of objects designed for their comfort that now bruised flesh. Behind it trains all over the line stopped between stations, no doubt, delaying appointments, breaking promises, bending the people of Leiodare to its will.

Eugenio helped the conductor off the track and hurried to the exit. Just outside the station, a black bird circled overhead— noticed by first one commuter, then another. They stood, mouths agape, pointing into the darkness. The giene lights lit them up so that they seemed people frozen in a blast.

Eugenio hailed a taxi and hopped in. He couldn't help but stare out the window, gnawing at the nail on his index finger. With all that Leiodare had built to hold back the night, still here the unfathomable came on wings not seen so openly in the city in decades. As Eugenio watched, the birds beat their bad omen through the sky.

When he reached their home, Eugenio tore though the place looking for Lucine. He found her in her workshop. An array of parts scavenged during Lucine's time at The Dumps covered the work table in front of her: small metal calipers fashioned from the tines of a silver serving spoon, a handful of bearings, a broken convection unit, several digicom casings, tiny solar cells, and more. Behind her dozens of completed tools hung neatly across the vast wall. In her hands, Lucine held a small schematic that she compared to the parts in front of her. Eugenio's entrance seemed to have interrupted her in mid-thought. The mini recorder lay next to her right hand.

"The key to finding the right tool—" she began.

Eugenio walked into her workshop, feeling worse for the wear. Lucine looked up, already smiling at him. She stole a glance at his hands. He knew that the tip of his left index finger was raw and red.

"Troubles, Eu?" she asked, putting down her schematic.

"Birds," he began, out of breath. "Birds loose in the city."

"What?" she said, turning her full attention on him.

"Birds, I just saw birds."

"Eu, could this be your—"

"No, it's not in my head. It's not the anxiety. It's fucking birds all over the city. Dozens of them, maybe hundreds. I counted twenty-six just on the way here."

Lucine jumped up from the workbench and went to the window, an excited smile on her face.

"Twenty-six?!"

"Yes," he answered.

"Finally, it's time." She looked over at her tools anxiously, mumbling to herself. "It will just have to do; I'll make them work."

Eugenio leaned against the table and for once just asked straight-out. "What are you planning, Lucine?"

"Every cage has its key, Eu," she answered.

"What does that mean?" he demanded. "Elaborate."

"You'll see soon enough," she said playfully.

Eugenio smiled ruefully. It faded quickly. The worry lines reappeared on his forehead.

"Eu," she said. "Don't worry. Emergency Management will send out their battalions with their nets and guns and that will be the end of it."

"And then what? They're wrong about how this started. So how can they ever hope to fix it, or evolve beyond it? It's a problem that must be resolved. Now. They still think the root was rational, that the thought the birds were spreading the disease and that's why the slaughter was necessary."

Heat crept into Eugenio's face and he felt spittle collect at the corners of his mouth. He took a deep breath.

"Why then?" Lucine asked.

"They would tell you that the birds are to blame, that their own sordid past made them targets. They've always been a vector for disease."

"A given," Lucine said; her attention darted back to the collection of odds and ends laid out on the counter. "That seems reason enough for them to have behaved the way they did."

"It's not the reason though. I used to think that too, but something's changed my mind," Eugenio said.

"Yes?" She waited.

"I'd been reexamining the vid links and broadcasts from that time. There were the broadcasts you'd expect. You've seen the initial report that they always dig up around the commemoration, the one where they first reported the risk of infection. And then not long after the cameras kept rolling on an empty studio because they'd all become infected during the first week of twenty-four-hour coverage."

"Yes, of course," Lucine replied. She retrieved a bag from the back of the door and began to pack her tools.

"That one was bad, but there were other images, ones that started on that station, and then others picked up and rebroadcast.

Those they don't talk about so much now, but during those three months, stations broadcast literally thousands of images of birds on bodies. Not just vultures as one might expect, but all kinds of birds. And even some rare cases of vulture attacks when people tried to shoo them away."

"Attacks?"

"It's unpleasant," he said, hesitating. Lucine pursed her lips and looked at him. He continued.

"Apparently they have corrosive vomit," he said.

"Enough." Lucine shook her head in disgust. "So the extermination?"

"The extermination. Probably at the very beginning they believed the birds were the cause."

"And later?"

"Later they knew better. Or should have. McClaren Industries had something to do with it."

"How do you know?" she asked.

"I found something at Meta. An old record on an iCDC subdirectory. Peter Warrel—Patient Zero—had been attending a McClaren conference and if McClaren Industries was involved, someone at the city knew something. That company has bankrolled half of Leiodare; back then they traded personnel constantly. And already reports from the iCDC had started to come online within a month. Their reports talked about probable causes and resolution scenarios, directives, precautions, all of it. Continuing the extermination, the ban, was just resentment. And rage," Eugenio said.

"Rage lasts twenty-five years?" Lucine asked.

"Resentment certainly can," Eugenio said. "And I think iCDC might have known it. Why keep the city quarantined for so long? Most of the infected population died within six weeks. The extra time was just caution on the part of iCDC and the surrounding city-states. Or maybe they wanted to see how resultant Leiodaran stress disorders would play out. I don't know."

"What would your colleagues say about this theory?" Lucine asked.

"They don't care. They just want bug reports—and obedience. But I'm right. I know I am. And there must be something else."

"Why?" Lucine asked.

"They didn't even review the files I sent them. Even intellectual curiosity would make you review them and my boss looked uncomfortable. Director Vaughn—he's an imperious bureaucrat, but Lena is a scientist and she said not one word about the files."

"Reason is often too easily defended. Actions garner reactions." She loaded the last tool into her bag and threw it over her shoulder, looking ready and excited.

"Let's go fix this," she said.

None of this changes Lucine's plans, Eugenio thought, not his bosses' refusal to hear the truth, nor the birds. No change to her plans at all. Not even his failure. Lucine had had the better plan all along as it required no one else. Crestfallen, Eugenio turned his head searching for something to distract him from the stinging in his eyes.

She grabbed his hand. When he looked up he could see the thin scalpel she held, small drops of blood already dripping from her hand. Tears threatened to well again, but this time for a different reason. Clenching his jaw he watched her cut him slowly and relished the fire moving across the edge of his palm as the scalpel separated his flesh, opening him to his sister. He took her bleeding hand to his face and sucked the red away as she took his bleeding finger into her mouth. Already the ritual began to center him as she had known it would.

"Flesh of my flesh," Lucine said.

"Blood of my blood," he continued.

"Time to leave, Eu. Time to fix the city."

Eugenio, still holding her hand, squeezed gently.

"How?"

"We're going to dismantle the fence, Eu, and let all these trapped souls go free," she said.

13

An alert tone chimed through Rory's rooms, the three-note melody he had reserved for one algorithm only. He wrenched himself away from the McClaren Industries files he'd been poring over, and took a swig from his glass of whiskey.

"Report on. Maximize," Rory said. He stood in his bathrobe and bare feet, and walked to the great room to see the image that filled the center of its immense screen. The giant holo head of a female newscaster hovered over the divan.

"Reports have surfaced of an avian invasion in downtown Leiodare," she began.

Rory's heart started beating again. He exhaled brusquely and felt oxygen flow back through his diaphragm. He'd set the algorithm to alert him to reports that involved the words "exodus," "evacuation" or any major population disruptions in the city. This must have pinged population disruption.

"So far there's been no determination of whether the birds—reportedly in the hundreds—are a domestic terrorist attack or a foreign contagion. The city has assured us that the rumors that the birds are smuggled domestics is wholly untrue. Emergency Management has not yet confirmed, but sharpshooters could be deployed at any moment. We've also received reports of two trans fires in The Dire where members of the Starlings are suspected of arson. Right now, we have exclusive live video from the Wiley's Tasty Treats advercam in The Dire—"

"Report mute," Rory said. The talking head continued in pantomime. "Report minimize."

It shrank to the size of Rory's own head and continued on as he walked through the image and over to the window that faced the shopping district next to The Spires.

Could it be true? Birds openly in the city and so many of them? This did not seem some lark of the Starlings or an underground aviary raided in retribution from a rival supplier. If the report was to be believed the city protocol was to evacuate. He'd read it a dozen times in the annual report. If they did, maybe he could—

Rory would not finish that thought. The disappointment might be more than his meds could handle. And regardless, he had important work to finish. He had to find out how McClaren Industries had been involved in the epidemic that destroyed his family. Not quite sure he was ready for that revelation, he paused and took a seat on the chaise lounge. For a few deep breaths, Rory lost himself in the twinkling lights of the night skyline as he watched billowing clouds pass by in the moonlight and wondered what news, from outside and in, the next few hours might bring.

Slowly he got to his feet and returned to the library. Inside mounds of loose papers and disks dotted the floor. He had started by methodically searching through and diligently replacing the files that he'd already reviewed, but as he dug deeper, this system had begun to devolve into tossing files into various piles, leaving a few stragglers in the middle of the floor. Moving a few of them out of his way as he walked to the other side of the room, Rory settled back into his overstuffed leather chair and an archive of paper records he'd kept in the back closet.

He turned to the stack of red research and development portfolios resting on an ottoman near the chair and began again in earnest. He opened the one on top and scanned for the names of the men and women he'd known to run the low-profile, high-yield projects that his grandfather had coveted.

"The dirt under the foundation," Pop Pop called them. Those kinds of projects were most likely to be well hidden, and usually for good reason. He was sure he'd find something significant in these files. But beyond a few suspicious financial disclosures, there was nothing relevant in the first portfolio, or the second. He quickened his pace.

In his haste Rory quickly transformed the library into a mess of half-truths and financial alchemy strewn in every corner. But still, everything he found was industry standard and totally unrelated to infection. Tapping his fingers on his knee, he turned to the gig files on his home machine and began loading them in, at first autoscanning for key phrases, but soon after this yielded no results Rory skimmed them himself, seeking out signatures instead of names. Perhaps what had been endorsed would be more telling than what was assigned. The members of research and development were a proud group, frequently arrogant, but smart—only a few would be remiss enough to put their signatures on files that might come back to haunt them. He would start by trying to cull them first.

But when he finally found the link he'd been searching for—a battery of diagnostic test results that clearly showed the same contagion that would come to be called the Crumble—the e-signature wasn't of the supervising head, but the last person who had opened the file. The name was foreign to him, and he could find no record of it anywhere in the McClaren files, a pirate's name of Bly—someone who'd never worked for McClaren as far as he could tell, but had stumbled on the file, it seemed, by mistake, searching for information on ways to amplify shared reals.

Rory sat with one hand covering his mouth, two fingers trembling against his lips. His gaze sank from the screen down to his lap. McClaren Industries had known there was a connection between the Crumble and their products. He needed to know more.

Pulling his chair closer to the reader, Rory began to click and slide his way further into the company's secrets.

There were too many products launched and shelved as a result of the conference to track down, but he did find one singularity: Peter Warrell. Buried deep in encryption and biometrics keys only a McClaren could possess, he found the files he'd been searching half the night to find. They were compressed together in a locked .axe file piggybacked one onto the other. They should have been deleted but the bin had been corrupted and so there they all sat in a tiny external drive, plain as a narrative.

Peter Warrel had been the lead bioengineer on Series 3 of the bridging software between The Last Word and VR applications, a key shareholder in the first series of virtu. He was the main designer of the discontinued Series 3. Digesting this information, Rory thought of the antique Series 3 rig he kept in a case in the living room. It had been discontinued after a single sales season. Apparently it had not been discontinued quickly enough.

"Not before it spread—" Rory's words caught in his throat as the next file opened. According to the files glowing in front of him, Contagion 142 had not been spread in the rigs. It was a byproduct of them.

McClaren Industries had caused the epidemic that annihilated his family and a sizable portion of the population those many years ago.

For several seconds, there was just silence, a stupefied paralysis that slowly worked its way out from the center of him. As it did every muscle in Rory's body contracted, until all of him clenched. When there was nothing left to squeeze, he shook. His eyes filled with tears that would not fall and a high, hurt sound pulled itself out of his chest, slowly, painfully. Alone at the top of the city, Rory keened.

14

In Anna's dream, Seife smiled at her from the bank of the River Ruelle. Mist hung over the water and as she walked closer to Seife, the mist grew denser, turned gray. It started to gather behind her and when she turned—

Smoke filled Anna's nostrils as she struggled to take a breath, and coughed herself awake. She bolted up in bed. A strange noise filled the room and it took her a moment to recognize the until-now unheard squawks of the cygnets from the giene spa. But there was more noise. She separated the swans' voices from the din of wood creaking and burning, bricks popping. The orange glow of fire lit up the space under the front door. No alarms sounded.

She grabbed her bag from the floor, stuffed a few soft items inside and rushed to the giene spa. Inside, the swans flapped their tiny wings uselessly and squawked. Anna scooped them out of the tub, along with the bags of damselflies she'd brought up that morning and placed them all gently in her bag. The egg, still wrapped in old t-shirts, went in next to them.

Her wall of work faced her and for a moment Anna stood frozen. All of her drawings would burn. Out in the hallway something came loose from its moorings and fell to the floor, perhaps through it from the groaning and crash that followed. She grabbed the tiny portrait of her mother she'd made the summer of virtuoso indoctrination, and left the giene spa.

Outside her front door, smoke filled the hallway. She didn't have to open the door to see the fumes crawling in from under.

She pushed the living room window open and stepped outside. A second later she'd carefully tightened the straps on the bag and was down the fire escape ladder to chart a new course, this time without the comforting voices of her past, but perhaps with something better. After all, this was only the second unlucky thing to happen to her since the cygnets had come and even magic couldn't stop a fire once ignited.

15

The small dome of Post One rose above the surrounding trees, a moonlit mound beckoning from the shadows. The night sky, a crisp and deep indigo, stretched out in the rarefied air above the building, the last fresh air before the silent, invisible threat of the fence. If not for the mounds of birds on the other side of the barrier it would be impossible to know the fence stood just a few hundred meters away.

Eugenio and Lucine approached from the northwest, careful to skirt the tree line before they moved into the open. On the way, Lucine had explained to him how the fence operated.

The fence worked as a two-stage system. A pair of invisible shells fifty meters apart surrounded the city. If one could see them from above, they would form a concentric circle. Lucine had paused here and looked at him significantly. The larger outside perimeter identified what passed through it. When it detected a bird that message was sent to the second barrier which then electrified to kill.

In the first few years of the barrier there had been two major problems. At first, the outer barrier malfunctioned. It began targeting not only avian DNA, but all uncategorized small endothermic animal DNA. This resulted in the near-eradication of two apparently new subspecies of jungle mouse, and had been repaired over a period of months. In the second incident, the inner barrier had been set at a lower stun-level voltage and dazed birds came careening into the city in droves.

Reports of mobbing and erratic behavior abounded. Both of these incidents happened in the first two years of operation. Leiodare recovered and improved their systems to the nearly self-maintaining fence in use today.

"So," she had explained, "there's only one way to disable it."

"What's that?" he had asked.

"Do exactly as I say."

As they approached the exterior of the building, Eugenio planned on doing exactly that.

The post seemed empty, but perhaps it was better staffed than the rest of the city. Eugenio played lookout while Lucine darted over to the windows. She looked in and motioned to him. Quietly, they climbed the stairs up to the office. Still, Eugenio's footsteps echoed on the metal and he winced, almost expecting to see someone to come out and investigate. Looking in the slitted window in the door, he saw an empty control panel and lit room; no one was inside it. Eugenio listened for anyone who might be just out of view. The wind over the treetops and the distant crackle of a fire somewhere reached him, but nothing else. Satisfied that they were alone, Lucine crossed to the entrance and stepped into the building.

Stone covered the doorway arches and floors. Plexi and high-sheen plastics covered every other surface for a disjointed effect. A bank of monitors and a sleek control panel were situated on Lucine's left. She walked to the seat in front of the panel, took out her tools, and went to work on the panel. Eugenio joined her there.

Lucine removed the facing and looked down at a circuit grid lit up yellow and blue.. She took out the makeshift soldering pencil in the small recess of her bag and began burning out lights in the grid; sharp fumes floated up .

"Can I help?" Eugenio asked.

She looked over at him, and put down the soldering pencil.

"Yes," Lucine answered, pulling a pair of cutters from her bag and handing them to him.

"See that relay there?" She pointed inside the panel, but Eugenio couldn't see much difference among the myriad wires and plastene chips.

"Which one?" he asked.

"That one there." She placed her finger near a blue wire curled around a yellow one.

"Yes."

"You'll need to cut it, remove it from this panel and solder it to the negative here in B Panel." She gestured to the panel below the counter. "I'll disconnect the negative, but in the meantime just cut the wire and don't let it touch the rest of the panel."

Lucine disappeared under the panel. Eugenio heard the noise of tools going to work underneath him. He jimmied the cutters into position and snapped through the wires. The lights in the room flickered.

"Eu?" Lucine asked.

Suppressing a curse, he answered.

"I cut the yellow too," he said.

"It's fine, just hold it free of—"

Wires in hand, Eugenio leaned down to listen. Blue wire met diode and the lights went out.

"Shit. I shorted the room," Eugenio said.

A pool of bright yellow light clicked on under the panel.

Lucine popped out from underneath. She held the torch in her hand.

"We'll fix it," she said calmly.

"I shorted the lights out in the whole post, didn't I?" Eugenio asked.

"The city, Eu," she answered.

He felt suddenly sick. Eugenio's handheld sounded.

"It can be fixed," Lucine said. "Answer it."

The phone kept ringing. "Eu," she said.

Eugenio clicked the "Accept" button and held the handheld to his ear.

"Dr. Oliveira." He didn't recognize the voice on the other end. "This is Rory McClaren. I've something for you. Come to The Spires. I have the tech you're searching for, the old virtu tech that created the Crumble."

The tourists wearing skimpy costumes and smeared face paint. Some of them still had their virtu rigs on.

"I'm on my way," Eugenio said, and hung up. He paused, trying to fully comprehend what Mr. McClaren had said. *The old virtu tech that created the Crumble.* Not spread the Crumble—created it.

"I have to go," Eugenio said. "McClaren called. Something unbelievable has happened." Eugenio saw the concern on Lucine's face and chose his words carefully.

"I'll be fine, Lucine. I'll meet you back as soon as I can."

She looked at him steadily, her lips slightly pursed.

"OK, Eu. You come back," she said.

Eugenio turned to leave.

"Eu?"

"Yes?" he asked turning back to Lucine from the doorway.

"You come back. OK?" she said. Her eyes amber in the torch's beam, her hands capable and ready to right so many years of wrong, Lucine could not have been more powerful or compelling. And still, she thought of him. Eugenio smiled despite himself.

"Of course," he said.

Outside, nearly all of Leiodare was now invisible in the darkness. Only The Spires remained alight. Wind beat near Eugenio and he jerked his gaze up, sure a black bird wing had passed though he couldn't see it. Instead of dark flying shadows his gaze met another sight rarely seen: endless points of scintillating light more lovely than any tower. Eugenio walked toward the stars hanging over the darkened city.

As he neared the edge of The Dire, strange outlines began to glimmer in the darkness. The outlines fit the forms of people. Limbs and heads were clearly demarcated even in the darkness. They moved as people did, each at their own pace, on their own route. Eugenio spied a half-dozen more smokey gray outlines on the next block, and more toward the edge of the tree line, as well as the intimation of more in all directions. He wondered how many were people, and how many spirits, though it mattered little now.

"Soon now, you'll all be free," he whispered as he took his handheld out of his pocket and recorded the images for his sister. "Lucine will make sure of that."

Tingling with anticipation and the charge of what he had seen, Eugenio headed off toward the glow of The Spires.

16

Morning found Rory, head in his hands, quiet and grim as the truth he had discovered. The Series 3 virtu rig rested at his feet where he had let it slip from his hands. He'd slept in the chair for a few hours, but he was again trying to understand how he and his family had let it happen.

At the time, the family had been told the tech was unreliable and that that was the main reason McClaren Industries decided to go nano, instead of bio, with future virtu rigs and reals. They'd thought no more of it than any other update at the quarterly board meetings.

They'd thought nothing of it and look what it had done to them.

He felt devoid of all emotion, empty. His body however was not quite so. Rory stood and slowly made his way to the giene spa to relieve himself. As he left the giene spa he glanced outside and stopped in mid-stride. The sight outside drew him to the plexi. From where he stood, his forehead pressed up against the plexi, he saw the streets emptying.

Emptying.

He took a deep breath as he began to rouse. Surely, they would soon start to come back. There had been quasi-evacuations before—tropical storms, infrequent hurricanes, once even a particularly productive bee year, but the people of Leiodare had always returned. Each time, they dashed his hopes of going outside into blessedly empty streets, of going home. In fact, they never really left, only clogged up the trains, the roadways,

and underground giene stations. In less time than it took for
Rory to enjoy a virtu he'd look back outside and see people
moving back into the city, his hopes dimming with each new
person on the street. And it couldn't be nearly as many people
leaving as it seemed to be. Rory sighed and turned back to
the library, glanced at the clock, and wondered how much
longer it would take Oliveira to arrive. He switched on an
archival performance of Annie Lennox, contemplated opening a bottle of wine.

After three glasses of vintage cabernet and a virtual
kayaking trip from Chaiwan's northeast shore to Okinawa,
Rory took a look outside. The city must have commandeered
the floating billboards—instead of innocuous ads for tooth-
paste and rejuvenation treatments, now emergency messages
scrolled down the screen just above the increasingly empty
streets. If they cleared out more he would continue considering. The idea of the big emptiness began to make its way out
of his heart and into his bones; soon it would want to tweak
his muscles into action.

Rory watched for twenty more minutes and counted less
people still. He called Oliveira to track his progress—closer but
not close enough. Drinking the last of the cabernet he decided
to count people like thunder. Each time a person crossed from
the northeast corner of Martin and Jackson he would count
off the seconds until the next crossing. Once he hit fifteen seconds, he went to retrieve his jacket and emergence kit from its
home in the armoire. He removed the new hearing aids and
replaced the old ones he was wearing. Next, Rory packed the
antique virtu rig and files of evidence in a case, placing it all
on the kitchen counter with a note for Oliveira.

Rory walked the perimeter of the room. Nose centimeters
from the glass, he surveyed the scene below, the newly emerged
patches of sidewalk, the things that people left behind in their
haste—errant clothing, indistinct black dots that Rory took

to be handhelds or some other digi flotsam. Though he tried his best to dispel the notion with waiting and further tests, there was still no surge of return. The suffocating bodies did not fill the streets.

Still it could happen. He counted twenty seconds on three corners and decided on a route. Out of habit, Rory grabbed his virtu rig. Seeing it in his hand though he slammed it down in disgust; then, after a few anguished seconds, picked it back up. Rory fiddled with the controls, consciously stopped his hand from switching up and instead went sideways. "Record," as foreign as Cantonese, glowed in the lower left-hand corner. He stood at the plexi between him and the anteroom. This time, his hand didn't hesitate at the lock, as he had twenty-five years ago. Rory took one last reassuring glance at the empty streets and the items he'd left for Dr. Oliveira, entered the unlock code and stepped into the private elevator that would take him away.

On his way down the elevator shaft, smooth and soft as a raindrop's trip to the ground, Rory bit back his anxiety, counting backwards in his head and stopped his hand from reaching up and punching the button that would take him back upstairs. Even the weight of the emergence kit in his hand didn't calm him. The elevator landed softly at the bottom while he tried to remember enough Italian to count back in that language. The doors slid back and opened onto the lobby.

Nothing was as he remembered. Not that he had suspected it. Somehow he'd forgotten the lobby's very existence. Upstairs, he had thought of the world outside the window and his rooms, but rarely of the people in that very building and never of its communal spaces. Now as he stood at the open doors looking out, Rory saw, just for a flash, what the lobby had once looked like by seeing all it was not: It was no longer burgundy. The plushness of the couches, the deep textured curtains and gold vases in the corners had been replaced by sunlight pouring in everywhere from the two-story-tall plexi walls. A warm wooden floor glowed in the light. And above it, polished basketball-size spheres like molten steel hovered in the air. All of it came across as retro as anything Rory could remember from his childhood.

Across the lobby, a well-dressed middle-aged man stood behind the counter, staring out on the street with his back to Rory. A doorwoman stood at her station near the door; she turned her head slightly and watched Rory approach. The man, ostensibly the concierge, watched the building across the street, not noticing him. At the station, Rory pulled a small package out of his pants pocket and placed it on the corner of the podium the doorwoman stood behind.

"Please give this to Dr. Eugenio Oliveira when he arrives."

She blinked and stared at him, realization now intensifying her gaze.

"Mr. McClaren?"

With a small smile, Rory turned away from her and toward the exit. The front door slid noiselessly open and he took a hesitant step out into the day. Even before the noise, he noticed the wind blowing gently across his face. It carried a smell with it. It was the first smell in years that he couldn't identify simply because he had not created it.

Rory breathed deep as he scanned the street—no one within twenty-five meters of him, the sunlight warming him. He moved quickly lest something go wrong. That first step felt as good as anything he could remember, as if the world had been born in that moment and not him back into it. Around him he heard the sound of people but could not see them. Distant voices melded together, creating a soft roar. Rory walked away from the roar and toward his old street.

On the corner where his family's house stood, a dozen Starlings dressed in their emblematic red boots talked and laughed. Luckily Rory had seen them first and been able to skirt the group without being noticed. After the last few blocks, he'd had a lot of practice avoiding direct contact with anyone. From the safety of the darkened doorways birds and from behind newsstands, Rory had watched people running from and the small fires that had broken out. He had overheard the arguments about whether stragglers would be locked in the city, saw the fights erupt over the smallest trespass, the slightest delays, had even witnessed a different group of Starlings toss a Molotov cocktail into a battalion trans without a single look back. For that reason, as much as any other, he gave the Starlings on the corner a wide berth as Rory made his way to the front door of the old family home.

He hadn't known he would come straight here, but as he found himself following the path home, it came as no surprise. It was the first time he'd had enough clearance to make it from The Spires to McClaren Street. He stopped at the stoop of their old building, afraid to look up and somehow see his nieces standing there, or his mother, or worse yet his sister Katherine. How he had loved Katherine.

See there, Rory thought, still outside and already it all starts to fall out of its hiding place. He briefly considered turning and continuing down the street, making a nice loop and then back to the penthouse. The thought in and of itself was irritating; he didn't have the strength to pretend that was possible. He had finally come home and fear would not make him leave.

After a moment's hesitation, he climbed the stairs and put his right hand on the palmlock. With his left he placed the old key in the deadbolt and turned. As Rory pushed the door open, it creaked on old hinges, not rusted, but not quite used to moving either. His entrance kicked up a thin layer of dust. He sneezed and stepped into the marble foyer. He felt an instant pang when he saw the rosette pattern in the floor. Rory had dreamed of it, had it incorporated into the drapery of his bedroom without realizing why. Standing here it seemed impossible that he could forget where the pattern came from. The floor loomed up at him and he had to steady himself against the wall.

Rory recovered and pushed off the wall, walked slowly into the family room beyond the foyer. Dust coated the back of his throat. Even to him, his footsteps sounded too loud in the space.

His mother's English chestnut shelves still lined the walls, each one floating independently and neatly stacked, allowing just enough room to accommodate the largest book on the shelf and no more. The old sofa still sat across from the shelves. The arm of the overstuffed sofa's green had faded to a lime color Rory felt certain she would despise. He looked over at the wall opposite and saw the cause of the faded couch. A folding wooden shade stood partly open; apparently it had been open for years. The area of hardwood from the window to the sofa had also faded from sunlight. Perhaps it had been open from the beginning. Maybe Katherine had looked out this window and down on to the street as she talked to him on the handheld that day.

Under his breath, he cursed the company that had closed the house up, then remembered he had given instructions to go only where the work required—still a simple matter of closing a shade.

Rory walked to the window, intending to close it himself, but it seemed pointless now; the damage had already been done. He stopped short and stepped over to the bookcase. On the far corner of the second shelf a small wooden frame caught his eye. The frame held a picture of the girls poring over the huge paper dictionary his mother had kept in the library. He held the photo up to his face, hand shaking. Energy flooded back into him and, almost impossibly, it felt as good as he had imagined it would feel. There had to be more photos upstairs. Rory turned and hurried in that direction.

His hand pushed dust down the banister as he grabbed it and pulled himself upstairs. The photos would be in his mother's bedroom on the maid's floor. She had always called it such though only she lived on that floor. He could hear her voice now, "I like to feel nestled, Ruairí." The bright blue of her door had not faded. He grabbed the knob and turned, half expecting to hear her call from her bathroom.

The door opened to blackness and a musty odor that hit Rory like a slap: the dank smell of mold and a coppery something he couldn't quite place. Rory pulled out the flashlight he'd brought and pointed it in the room. The strong mix of smells burned in the back of his throat and within seconds, the beginnings of a headache gathered behind his temples. The dark swam in front of his eyes. Roy blinked to clear his head, and drew back the hand that held the flashlight to cover his nose and mouth.

Rory knew instinctively that something lived in the dark. He stood in the hallway trying to decide if he wanted to meet it. Was that a tremor there at his feet? He thought he felt something move on the floorboards deep in the room and swung his flashlight towards it, cane held tightly as a baton in his other hand. A small rat emerged from his mother's bathroom and shot past him into the hallway. Rory grunted and jumped out of the way just in time to feel its tail smack his ankle. It took a few seconds for his heartbeat to slow down and in that time a second rat a bit slower and larger than the first bounded past him, out the door. This one was followed by a single bee that flew straight into Rory's face. He swatted it away and shone his flashlight into the darkness of the room.

The beam swept over a cloud of heavy mist on the other side of the cavernous room, but Rory didn't see any more rats. He swung the beam up towards the ceiling searching for bats, and across the floorboards again looking for rolling or scorpion beetles. The air grew prickly. Small hairs on his forearms rose up. His hearing aids emitted a small sound like feedback and Rory stopped cold where he stood. Breath left him. His senses locked in and stilled. He swung the flashlight towards the cloud of mist.

The swarm of bees was closer, no more than a couple of meters from him. Each bee looked indistinguishable from the next, a cloud bearing down on him. Rory stepped back from the door and slammed it hard on its hinge. He stood on the other side breathing heavily. When he felt a bit steadier, he hurried down the rickety flight of stairs and tried to figure out what to do next. He still wanted those photos.

Rory checked his satchel and moved toward the kitchen. He turned his hearing aids up to their highest level and almost deafened himself when he took a deep breath. Sonofabitch. He turned the volume back down, but not before registering a buzz from somewhere in the next room. He turned in time to see the first half-dozen bees.

Moving as quickly as the cane would allow him he was down the stairs and hallway. The buzzing grew louder and afraid to turn around Rory caught a reflection in a patch of clean on a dirty window. The buzzing cloud looked larger than it had just a moment ago. For all that his ears left him wanting, his eyes were as sharp as they'd been thirty years ago when he'd had them permanently corrected. And he could definitely see clearly enough to know that he didn't want to take another look. Rory grabbed the banister at the landing, and shot-put himself around it and the corner.

As he did, his foot caught on the landing and sent him sprawling. His elbow bashed into the glass in the front door, breaking a hole as big as his head. He'd take note of the gash later. For now he tried to pull his elbow out of the broken door, while causing as little pain as possible. The first bees were on him. He felt stings on the back of his head and an excruciating pain in his left eye. Rory moved, righting himself quickly and pushing himself through the door and outside.

His mind raced ahead of him, trying to come up with a viable escape route. He turned right, not quite sure of why. His security alert was as good as dead with no one on the other end, but he tried it anyway. He could feel the adrenaline pumping into his system, lubricating his creaky joints. His cane stabbed into the pavement sure as a rudder pushing him forward and past the group of Starlings he'd passed earlier. They looked at him quizzically at first and then behind him. Then they moved too. A couple of the small boys almost knocked him over in their haste. They scampered directionless. Rory had a plan.

The bees followed the group of Starlings and didn't seem to take much notice when he paused to catch his breath under a construction awning. Rory took this opportunity and slipped away, down a set of stairs to the subdoor of 28 McClaren Street, the family guesthouse. He found the right key and put his palm up to the lock. On his second try, he unlocked it, falling against the other side in relief.

A sudden debilitating round of coughing overtook him. He doubled over, his weight pressed against the head of his cane, focused on nothing but breathing for long, wheezing moments. Rory regained enough strength to straighten, though his heart still beat madly in his chest. Boxes filled the small storage room. Rory immediately began to check for openings in the room, turning up his hearing aid to listen for any telltale buzzing.

A scream rang out, momentarily deafening him. Rory lowered the volume of his hearing aid and hurried back to the door, cracking it open a few centimeters. He looked over the top stair and out onto the street. The Starlings seemed to have split up. The bees attacked a group of five. The group was left outside on the corner, a tall boy whirling around trying to swat away bees with his duster, three others did the same and there was a small figure on the ground. That one seemed to be unable to get up, whether from fear or injury Rory couldn't tell, but a small cloud of bees buzzed between Rory and the Starlings outside.

"Here!" he yelled. "Over here!"

He thought he saw the kid on the ground turn towards his voice. A flash of Katherine in the way she lay there. The others bolted towards him, rushing past him and into the room. With a curse, Rory walked outside. He moved as quickly as he could to the figure on the ground. The sound of buzzing had engulfed Rory's hearing aids. Already his vision was starting to narrow as the bee sting to his eye began to swell.

He reached the figure—a girl, he thought—and half-pulled, half-carried her to the top of the stairs. Bees stung his face, his neck, hands, and through his clothes. Within a few seconds Rory couldn't feel the stingers anymore and his world collapsed with his vision: there was the door to reach and nothing else.

He stumbled and nearly dropped her, and bashed his knee into the sharp edge of the stair instead. He opened his mouth to curse and bees choked him. He sputtered and stumbled again. The tall boy met them halfway up and helped get them inside. Rory handed the girl over to him and locked the door behind them. Only when he felt the lock hiss into place and the whisper of the seal engaging did Rory realize what he had done. He'd locked the door himself, and now he was trapped in this room full of people. The wheezing came back in small, panicked bursts.

The Starling who'd been on the ground kept screaming, making the dark blacker, the room hotter. A dozen bees buzzed around the room and the tall boy went about the business of swatting them down with his duster and immense hands.

Rory lit his flashlight, searching for a touchpad for the overhead lights. The kid stopped yelling, began to whimper. Rory thought perhaps it had been fear more than pain.

The sound of buzzing in the room began to fade as more bees were smashed against the floor and walls. Rory slid down the wall. He couldn't feel it; his back had gone numb same as everywhere else, but when he leaned back something stopped him from falling flat. His face burned. Besides the heat, it felt tight, ready to burst. The tall boy approached him and by the look on the kid's face, Rory was glad he didn't have to see what he looked like. Shock and mild disgust etched the tall boy's expression.

Rory'd planned on tasting a bit of freedom after all these years and now here he lay in a den of miscreants full of barbs and venom, his hearing aids making the sound of his anxious breathing as inescapable as the present situation.

The tall boy leaned down, his elbows on his knees, squinting into Rory's face, a low whistle escaped his lips.

"You're not gonna die, are you, old man?" he asked.

Even in his increasing stupor, Rory found the presence of mind to give the kid the finger. That should translate across the ages.

❖ ❖ ❖

Rory woke to an odd muffled sensation on his mouth. When he opened his eyes, the tall boy leaned over him pulling stingers out of his lips with his fingers.

"Don't move," the tall boy said, concentration knitting his eyebrows.

Rory couldn't but even if he could, he doubted he would. It had been too long since someone had touched him so intimately, with actual fingers and flesh—still Rory could barely feel it. His body felt like a hole he'd fallen into, everything seemed to be at a great distance. He could hardly feel anything at all and what he did feel was tight and hot. The soldier in him knew the stingers should be swept with a card, not plucked, but that would mean no touching, and in the back of his mind he knew it wouldn't last, this touching, so he closed his eyes again and tried to focus every bit of awareness on it, to wake up his comatose flesh and feel the preciousness.

It was nearly impossible. He felt a wreck. He pulled breath in on a rope of strength slipping from his grasp.

"Waste of time," a voice said. Rory wasn't sure it was wrong.

"Quiet," someone else said.

Rory opened his eyes to see who that was.

The kid that had been lying on the ground now stood a few meters from him. It was a girl, maybe twelve, he now saw, short and brown-skinned with disturbingly clear blue eyes that even he could see through the tunnel that his vision had become.

"He'll hear you," the small, blue-eyed girl said.

"Oh, excuse me, missus." An older girl walked into Rory's sight line and looked right at him. "Waste of time," she repeated, louder and slower this time.

Under other circumstances he might have considered her attractive. He could see himself contracting her for a virtu or two, a low-rung sex scan most likely. And in truth she'd only expressed how most of his virtuosos felt about him; still he decided she'd be best suited with disappointment and discomfort for long periods of time.

The small one threw a look her way.

"I'm sure that—" She looked at Rory expectantly. The tall boy stopped pulling at Rory's lips for a moment.

"Rory," he offered. He tried to remember the last time he'd introduced himself to anyone. Even before the Crumble people had known him on sight, as they did all McClarens. It was one of the reasons he'd joined the service, and started dying his hair black.

"You think I care 'cause he's got a name?" the shitty, pretty girl said.

"No, I wouldn't think you're quite capable of that," the small girl answered.

The tall boy stopped plucking at Rory's lips again, and turned to the girl nearest the door.

"Are they still out there?" he asked, resuming his task.

Rory heard the door crack open.

"Can't see. Can't tell," she responded.

"You might actually have to look outside. Two millimeters of light showing. Of course you can't tell," the small girl said.

"You think I'm going out there to—"

"Shhh!" Rory said. Surprised into silence the Starlings turned his way, but he only needed a second.

Rory briefly maxed out the volume on his aids.

"I don't hear them," he said.

"Oh well, let's just be on our way then. Pincushion coffin dodger's given the all clear," the rude girl said.

"Shut up," the small girl said. "If you don't like how this chattering does things, you should have stayed with Deed's group then. You're perfect for each other, pyros and psychos."

The rude girl hunched her shoulders and threw a sour expression at the floor, but she didn't speak.

The small girl walked over to the door and waved the timid one away. With a glance Rory's way she slowly opened the door and looked into the open space. After a few seconds, she stuck her head out, and more of her slowly disappeared outside. She closed the door with a soft click. The tall boy rose and hovered near the door. Just as he was about to follow her out, she reentered.

"We're clear," she said. "At least down to Mabach."

She walked over and helped Rory to his feet. The group crept out of the room. The tall boy took the lead, using his long limbs to wrap around the construction awning and peek out on the street's blind side. Flotsam from the evacuation blew in the breeze, but not much else stirred—no clouds of bees, not even an errant few. He motioned for the others to join him on the landing, and the ramshackle group inched their way back out on the street. Rory stood balanced between the small girl and the tall boy.

Pain broke through Rory's haze and he groaned quietly. It took an effort to lift his head and gaze down the street. He turned his head back to his family's home and caught the rude girl looking at him. The girl's face actually went a bit soft with concern.

Rory turned away from the house, and shuffled forward first, intent on exploring the lost blocks.

17

Flames had completely engulfed Anna's building. She slept in the rubble. Once the fire crews saturated the brownstone with foam, gel, and sand, even the smallest embers were soaked, posing no more danger than the dirt at Anna's feet. So she had carved a circle of softness where only the sand touched her. She left slivers of sight, holes in the makeshift walls where at near every height between lying and standing she could see what might approach.

The rest of the city still stood around her, but the ruins of her building seemed safer than the buildings and parks so recently, or perhaps only partially, deserted. The birds kept her company. She slept in fits and starts, waking to the sound of breaking glass, distant shouts, and alarms going off all over the city. She wrapped her arm around the bag that held the swans safely inside, and leaned against the remnant of an unscorched wall. Anna tried to pass out just long enough not to wake exhausted.

It had been years since she slept outside. The morning came strong and not so gradually as she remembered. First just twilight in the east, and then the next time she noticed, glaring daylight beat red behind her closed eyelids. The smell of smoke had lessened in the night and turned to that of char. She woke again coughing from what had built up in her throat. Her stirring set the swans to moving and, slowly, she stood up and looked around from behind her makeshift fort. Mc-Claren Street looked beaten. The street was empty. The other residents in her building had left with relatives or friends, made their way to the city-appointed temporary housing, or wandered away into the night. Just down the block, Logi's windows had been smashed, and the Municipal Rest on the corner also seemed to have lost a few of its own windows to bricks, and Anna hoped nothing worse. Guns were not permitted in Leiodare—of course, neither were birds.

Anna readjusted the small stun stick she'd kept in her inner pocket last night and scanned the streets, checking in all directions. She slowly looked around the block once more. Down near the Municipal Rest building she spied a pair of people approaching from the west. She crouched down behind the half-wall of rubble and squinted, trying to discern their nature. Absentmindedly, Anna reached out to the bag and gently laid a hand next to the swans inside; she felt them shift towards her. Their chirping quieted.

The one in front seemed to be a woman, smaller than her companion and with a lighter step. As she came closer, something in Anna unknotted and she stepped from behind her cover.

"Anna," Seife said.

Anna looked from Seife to the man approaching.

"It's OK. He's with me," Seife said.

"I know her," Seife said to her companion. "Anna, this is Makisig. He's a caller too," Seife explained, "and a friend."

Makisig extended his hand and flashed a smile. "The man in blue, pleased to know you." Anna took his hand, shook once, and brought her attention back to Seife.

Makisig looked from one to the other. He cleared his throat. "I'll check on the residents," he said, turning towards the Municipal Rest.

Anna shouldered her pack and walked over broken brick until she stood directly in front of Seife. She wiped some dust from eyes. Her gaze shot up and down the street before settling on Seife. A tired smile inched the corners of her mouth up a centimeter.

"No call this morning," Anna said.

"No," Seife replied quietly. Her jaw tensed slightly as she looked over the remnants of the building. As Anna turned almost the full way around to look behind her, a small sound escaped the large black pack on her back. Seife squinted and did a double take. Anna jerked back around. She saw the question in the other woman's expression, but Seife said nothing.

"They seem to be gone for now," Seife said slowly.

"Who?" Anna asked.

"The ones who did this," Seife answered, motioning at what was left of the building and the remnants of furniture that poked out from the wreckage. A single copper woman from the building's tower had been saved by some providence. A large black bird flew in from the east and landed there, on the tip of a finger pointing straight into the sky.

"Why are you out here?"

"We wanted to see for ourselves how things were—at least on the route. We see these people every day and sitting in Smoketown watching the broadcasts—well, it's better to see for yourself," Seife answered.

"I'm glad to see you're all right," Anna said.

"I'm fine. Smoketown's fine. The rest of the city could be better—and you," Seife responded. "You stayed here?"

"I live here," Anna replied.

"I know," Seife answered. "I mean you stayed here—after."

"It seemed the safest place," Anna replied.

"The safest place?" she said slowly. "You could have—"

A loud chirp was emitted from directly behind Anna.

"I could have?" Anna prompted quickly.

"You could have contacted me. You could have stayed with me. Or at a hotel or any number of places."

"Hunh," Anna said. This was the first time she'd considered that. "Well," she said a bit uncertainly, "This seemed safest."

The chirp reinsinuated itself in their conversation. Seife's eyebrows went up and she tilted her head slightly, waiting for Anna to explain. Anna stared back at her. The other woman exhaled slowly.

"Where will you go now?" Seife asked.

Makisig approached from behind.

"They're not there," he said.

Seife looked at him, alarmed.

"Who?" Anna asked.

"The residents of Municipal Rest," he answered.

"They were evacuated," Anna said. "Last night, after the fire."

"That sounds like a good idea. McClaren's not safe now. You are being evacuated today," Seife said, taking Anna by the hand and walking back to Makisig. Anna made no protest; still small chirps could be heard between their footfalls. Makisig looked back, and over at Seife. They shared a wordless exchange, and the three of them climbed into Makisig's trans parked around the corner.

As they approached Delphi Avenue, Anna saw a lone security officer run up the stairs to an old city administrative building where flames burst from the second and third-story windows, showering glass onto the pavers below. A small group of teenagers dressed in dark dusters and red boots came tearing round the back of the building and ran towards them. Starlings. One of them, a short boy with a shock of dyed red hair cut into a rooster's comb that streamed out behind him, stumbled and came careening towards the trans. His face smacked up against Seife's window, his grimace of surprise and pain smeared into the plexi only centimeters from her face. As he righted himself, the security officer ran up from behind and leveled a rifle at the kid, squeezing the trigger. Just as he did, a second Starling tackled him, knocking his aim off and the shot went wild, striking the trans' hood. The engine died. Anna moved without thinking. She opened the door and hit the redhead full in the back, sending him face-first to the ground.

"Fool! Maybe you can find a way of expressing yourself without killing us all," Seife said harshly. "You set your own city on fire! Imbecile!"

The redhead pulled out a homemade incendiary from his pocket and from his other pocket a trigger. Anna heard Makisig get out of the trans and start to move around to her side.

"No!" the other Starling shouted from the ground. He'd stunned the security officer, who now lay twitching on the sidewalk. The larger boy got shakily to his feet. Makisig hesitated and looked down at the redhead on the ground. Anna kept her attention on him, one hand on her stun stick.

The redhead reluctantly put away his toys and stood up, dusting himself off. He looked at Anna with open hostility and joined the other Starling.

"No quarrel here," the larger Starling said.

"Perhaps *you've* no quarrel," the redhead said, snarling up at his companion.

A scream rang out from the building. They all turned to the sound.

"Deed, I thought you said it was clear," the larger Starling said to the redhead as the group of them moved closer.

A man dressed in office attire staggered from the building. The left side of his short afro had been singed down so that Anna could see the arm of his eyeglasses through his hair.

The redhead guffawed. "I thought you said it was clear," the redhead mocked. He grinned widely, and choking back his laughter, took off running low across the lawn. He disappeared into a nearby alley.

The security officer struggled to get to his feet. The larger Starling saw him and ran in the opposite direction. An ambulance siren wailed in the distance.

"Will you two be OK?" Makisig asked the officer. He nodded his assent.

"We'll have to continue on foot," Seife said. Anna, Makisig, and Seife slowly walked away from the pair on the lawn as the siren came closer.

A small black bird flew above them, flying in long, slow ovals. Makisig turned his head up to follow its flight path.

"Let's take a short cut," he said. "Off the main thorough-fares."

Bird songs twittered through the city, insistent and surreal as a recurring dream. The sound of birds and the trio's footfalls disappeared and reappeared as they walked, drowned out by the disorder around them. The ground under their feet was uneven; abandoned bags and trash covered it, the things left behind tripping them up as they tried to reach Smoketown before dusk.

Seife spoke over her shoulder to Anna. "You have a secret. So do I. I'll tell mine first: The second-most-often-asked question I hear at donors' dinners is: how did you become a caller?"

Makisig made a small noise of assent.

"This is what I would tell them if they truly cared to know: When you burn something, what is left of it is free. It floats where it likes—between crevices, under locked doors, around obstructions that would stop every living thing with bones. When you burn bones what is left of them floats freer. It cannot be contained, but it can make you its container: You breathe it in and it's part of you. So we burn our bones at night, so we can't see the smoke. That way we can pretend that what we do is work—and not part of us. We pretend that we can walk away from it, wash it away in the shower, watch the grit swirl down the drain and go to sleep at night, seemingly as alone as we were that morning. No more bird than the day before, no less free."

She had Anna's full attention now.

"The only way you can burn hundreds of birds per week—pick up their delicate, beautiful bodies in shovels made especially deep to capture their wings and then put them out to bake in the sun—is not to ignore the clack of cracking bones, the stench of rotting wonder, or the insects that feed on the precious waste. The only way to live with this is to revere it. But you can't be arrogant and revere yourself. You revere their sacrifice, their magic, and your own bravery because you've allowed yourself to know beyond the convenience of denial that what you do is wrong. I knew it when I was a child working the mound and I know it now. Only then can you balance it.

"That is why in Smoketown, those of us who stay, often call. Imitation may be the sincerest form of flattery but to revere, you must do something more."

Makisig slowed his gait and turned around now to watch Seife quietly. He looked at her warmly and walked closer to her as she continued.

"In Smoketown, once they built bricks for Leiodare's nostalgic buildings; now we burn bones. So always Leiodarans have depended on us. But as in most things I leave the truth unspoken when they ask me. Why?" She turned to Anna. "Because the question I'm most asked at donor dinners is whether it's true that callers are gifted and understandably high-priced prostitutes."

Makisig laughed out loud, shaking his head. The noise set the cygnets off, their chirps clearly audible from Anna's bag.

"That's my secret: one of them anyway. I think I know yours," Seife said.

Anna stared at Seife in disbelief. How could she have known to say that? To share the guilt and the penance of the callers of Smoketown? Seife may have gotten the secret wrong, but perhaps not. Anna kept silent though a gnawing sensation began in her chest. She took a single long stride and pulled up flush with Seife. Anna dropped her shoulder and pulled the strap of the pack away from her, releasing it so she could swing the whole pack to her front. Opening the top flap she put one hand inside and the chirping quieted. Seife peered over, trying to get a better look. Anna opened a side pocket with her other hand and pulled out a few of the damselflies, and placed her hand back in the pack.

"Breakfast," Seife said. "This would be a good time for breakfast."

Makisig, Anna, and Seife rested under shade of a large mango tree and quietly ate its fruit. The black birds arrived in pairs, populating the branches above.

They reached the edge of Smoketown well before dusk. The sounds of the evacuation became more removed as distant exotic bird calls began to replace the sound. They walked past the African fusion restaurant, with its darkened lights, past the kilns and into the residential section. Underneath the nearest band of trees, a small group of people stood a few doors down talking animatedly. They gestured toward the city. As they approached the group, Anna could hear incoherent words cutting through the wind in the nearby trees. When people in the group saw Makisig and Seife they waved and several members hurried over.

"Where's your trans, Maki?" a brunette woman in green slacks asked.

Makisig laughed humorlessly. "It's resting. I'll get a tow later, if there's anything left of it."

"There've been reports of rioting," a young brown-skinned man said. Tall and handsome, the shape of his face looked familiar to Anna. He stood close to Seife and Anna couldn't mistake the resemblance.

"To say the least," Seife said. She hooked her arm briefly around his and squeezed his bicep. "My brother, Rene." She

nodded to Anna. "You might remember him from the club."
She opened her introduction up to the general group. "Everyone, this is Anna." They nodded.

"Rioting *has* begun," Seife continued. "And the Starlings
are out."

"You should have waited for me," Seife's brother said.

"Resting? What do you mean resting, Maki?" the brunette
asked. "What happened?"

"Starlings—" Makisig began.

"We'll leave you to tell the tale, Maki. Meet at your place
later?" Seife asked. Makisig nodded and started in on his story.

Rene followed Anna and Seife as they left the group.

"Don't do that again," Rene said.

"Rene—" Seife stopped. Anna looked over at the siblings,
saw the imploring in Rene's eyes. Seife softened her tone and
finished.

"I won't, Rene. You make the same promise."

"Done," he said. He nodded at Anna, raised an eyebrow
at his sister, and returned to the group.

Anna and Seife walked down the swept lane below the
houses to the last band of homes, those nearest the invisible
barrier. In the distance, the fence stood out clearly, defined
by what lay outside it—the emptiness of the drying plain, but
mostly by the birds.

A pile of birds, stiff with death, cascaded down the side of
the electric barrier. It looked like a wedge of black, blue, and
cream towards the top and a wide swath of desiccated white
and brown at the bottom. Apparently they couldn't cart the
corpses off to the baking plains quickly enough to keep the
pile from forming.

The flock followed Anna and Seife. They circled the grey
stacks of kiln smoke and immediately retreated to the trees
near the fence. The flock flew near the mound, squawking and
spreading their wings, sounding alarms that went unheeded

by the birds on the other side of the fence. They lay as still and dead as they'd been before the flock arrived. Anna looked up to the flock and wondered how long they would stay.

Anna's gaze drifted over to the mound, mesmerized by the simple horror of it.

"I thought the fence only stunned them," Anna said.

"The fence stops them—sometimes stunned, sometimes dead. But always stopped," Seife replied.

"You just leave them piled up like that?" she asked

"Usually, no. But lately it has been particularly busy. It's migration season. When the birds—"

"I know what migration season is," Anna said absent-mindedly. She continued staring at the birds.

"Yes. You must," Seife answered. She pointed up at the nearest home, just above them. A long horizontal window crossed from one side of the building to the next. From it, a warm yellow light fell on the shoots and tiny ferns at their feet.

"My home," Seife said. "Please come inside."

Anna climbed the stairs behind Seife. The swans were now quiet on her back, probably sleeping. Up above them the sky was clear and blue, the green around them alive with the sound of bird songs.

Seife's house looked much larger on the inside. Most everything was made of wood and stone. To the immediate left, a half wall separated her bedroom from a large open living space of perimeter couches and an overstuffed sectional. An antique stereo cabinet took up the other wall of the open living space. Her bedroom space faced an open slate floor and a large kitchen with floor cabinets and kitchen table covered in a bright red tablecloth. Light filled up the room and two large ceiling fans kept a cool breeze circulating around the room. The open windows let in the sound of the jungle beyond the perimeter. Anna stood at the entrance, trying to take it in, but her gaze had stopped at the second couch. She roused herself.

"Do you have a tub?" Anna asked.

"Water closet's in that corner and the showers downstairs, under the house." Seife pointed. "But no tub, I'm afraid." She looked at Anna a bit quizzically.

"For the cygnets," Anna replied. "In my bag."

"I'm sure we can find something," Seife said and stepped back out, stopping just outside the door. "I will be back soon. Have a seat."

Anna heard her bound down the stairs.

She walked to one of the couches and sat down heavily. As she sunk into the thick padding, her legs gave up their battle to keep her upright and her left thigh began to twitch as the aches and pains from the last twenty-four hours began to register. She leaned over, resting her head on her forearms and took a deep breath. Anna couldn't remember the last time she felt so tired. Even doubles at the warehouse, running up and down ladders and loading gear hadn't left her this weary, she couldn't remember what had—even wandering in the forest.

She took the pack gently off and spied in on the cygnets. Sure enough they seemed to have fallen asleep; they'd need to eat when they woke up. She'd have to find something, but not quite yet. She had at least a few moments to herself. Anna placed the bag on the floor and started to take off her boots. Thinking better of it, she moved closer to the edge of the couch and hung her feet over the edge as she stretched out. Her eyelids drifted closed.

Yelling woke her. Disoriented, she tried to remember where she lay. Wooden table, stone floor, leaves through the window. Not until she saw her sullied boots did it come back to her. The cygnets still slept in the bag next to the couch. Seife had not yet returned.

"That can't be!" a woman's voice yelled.

"Just listen, Della! Listen!" someone responded. Anna could hear other muffled voices. She walked over to the kitchen window and peered out. Down below, fifteen or so people stood in a loose group around a young girl. Seife stood next to the girl with her arm protectively around her shoulders. Anna couldn't hear what the girl said, but judging from the group's facial expressions it made them uneasy, especially the brunette who had taken Makisig aside earlier. Seife looked up and saw Anna in the window. She nodded slightly, acknowledging her and joined back in the discussion. A few minutes later Anna watched Seife walk back toward her house. She turned to the door as Seife entered.

"What is it?" Anna asked when she came back in.

"Here," Seife said, motioning Anna outside. Anna joined her on the landing. A large metal tub waited at the foot of the stairs.

"It's one of Makisig's old planters. He says you can use it as long as you want." Anna glanced back toward the city, uneasily.

"What's happened?" Anna asked.

"The fires are spreading. The fire crews having trouble keeping up. And the electricity grid is still out."

"Starlings," Anna said.

"Perhaps not," Seife said. "Not the grid anyway. Vera is just back from The Shallows. She is a Starling. Well, she's from here, but she's been gone for a while. She was following some guy. Anyway, she's been running with them for months—and she says the electricity problems aren't because of the Starlings. And even given what I have seen today, I have my doubts as well. The grid's not the sort of thing you can firebomb with a homemade incend. If it were it would have been bombed a decade ago. I'll bet you a full stick that the grid is designed to withstand the common threat. I should know; every department in the city thinks alike, really it's all they're allowed to do. Even the Arts Guild with their security teams trailing us. They always guard against the most common threat."

"If the Starlings didn't do it, who then?" Anna asked.

"I wish I knew," Seife answered.

Anna nodded and walked back to the couch. She picked up the bag and joined Seife at the door.

The first group of people arrived while Anna and Seife sat next to the metal tub, watching the swans eat. Seife had brought some rolling beetles to supplement the last of the damselflies. She and Anna were deep in sleep-deprived discussion of which insect the cygnets would eat first. One of the swans gulped down a beetle struggling to move on the surface of the water.

"You see!" Seife said.

"Seife," a male voice called from behind them. They turned to find Rene approaching with a bag of medical supplies draped across his shoulder. Anna couldn't help noticing that the large red cross matched the shirt he wore.

"Little help? People are starting to trickle in from the city," he said.

Anna and Seife stood.

"No," Seife said. "You rest. I will return soon."

"I've heard that before," Anna said.

"As soon as I can, then."

18

All night Eugenio had had no choice but to scurry through the dark. Already Leiodare was a changed place—not because of bugs or superbugs, but because the lightless streets made Eugenio's home foreign and the people had begun to turn on one another. Besides The Spires, the only light came from small fires that the Starlings had set in the western half of the city.

In morning's dim rays he saw thin plumes of smoke in the distance rising beyond the Gardens. The hidden birds of The Dire cried out openly. It was an eerie sound to be heard this close to the Center. He continued on, slowing as he moved onto more crowded streets.

Road blocks had risen in The Dire. Just a few blocks up, battalions clogged the streets as they tried to beat back a horde of rolling beetles that spilled forth like a slow and menacing lava flow. It wasn't time for beetles to migrate, and broadcasts had reported the successful annihilation of their food source in this part of Leiodare, so this sudden surge meant that something had scared them into moving as one. Eugenio didn't like the idea of trying to imagine what could make a million of anything run. And in the entomological nightmare that Leiodare could be, given the right circumstances of unbalance and overcorrection, the possibilities were unfortunately numerous.

For the tenth time, Eugenio wished that he had driven, but it looked like many of the roads had already been restricted to emergency vehicles only. Protocol dictated that the city evacuate tourists first. Present circumstances certainly qualified.

Ahead of him a coupe jetted up and over the traffic clogging the streets. The patrol officers at the corner of the road block immediately went to their vehicle, waiting for the coupe to hit open street. When it did and no one was beneath them, the officers hit their kill switch and every engine on the street died. The coupe abruptly plummeted the fifteen meters to the ground. Though cushioned by its emergency thrust and bags, the thing still wrecked when it hit and chunks of impact foam flew out of the windows. The people inside would be straining to free themselves from cushioning as the officers stood outside the trans, looking beleaguered and unamused.

As if by providence, an unoccupied taxi turned the corner and Eugenio ran for it. Once inside, he directed the driver to The Spires.

"I set the price," the driver said, looking at him in the rearview mirror.

"Of course," he replied smoothly to her.

She turned off the main avenue and onto a side street. People packed the side streets as well. Here, the rush seemed to have a vein of efficiency moving through its chaos. People and trans shared the space as they moved to the west, ostensibly to the Jackson Arch, the formal entrance gate of the city. Individuals dodged around families and the obvious couples, swinging their hand-held belongings around obstacles. A woman on a motorcycle gunned her engine trying to get around the few trans on the roadway.

The people carried big bags, Eugenio noticed—not the usual stylish back pouch or parachute of rigid cotton, not even the tasteful backpack squares that usually covered upper backs all over the city. These packs covered their wearers' entire back down to the waist, and sometimes beyond. Ahead of the taxi, a young couple stepped off of the curb and almost into the path of the taxi. The driver swore under her breath.

Across the street, a building exploded. The force threw debris into the roadway, and the taxi's proximity alarm went off. Having detected danger of damage, it shuttered itself, reinforced metal vanes flowing into place. Duocrete chunks thumped against the sides of the vehicle as Eugenio braced for further impact. His ears rang in the darkness. The interior light wasn't working and so they endured the darkness until the thumping around them suddenly cut short. A light on the instrument panel lit up yellow, and the taxi went through its system's check. The external camera light blazed red—it'd been taken offline. They'd have to open the shutters to see. The driver hit the retract button. The shutters sank back into their recesses, and she and Eugenio peered out in the murk.

Eugenio could only see the dust that filled the air. Around them, the sound of coughing slowly replaced the noise of gravel landing. They would have to wait for it to settle before they could safely move forward. When it cleared, they saw that most everyone appeared to be moving; directly in front of the destroyed building, a middle-aged man with a blue scarf lay with his head in the gutter. From the unnatural angle of his neck, it didn't look like he had survived. As people scrambled to flee, what had been efficient turned frantic and broken. They drove grimly on.

The taxi driver stuck to the side streets as they entered the center of the city. The taxi separated from the long line of cars inching out of Leiodare. For a moment the taxi driver sat and watched the river of people surge away from them, then they continued on their way.

Nearer The Spires, the streets were quieter, emptier. The driver let him out a few doors down when a group of well-dressed businessman with frightened expressions appeared. They looked around spastically, with their briefcases held up in defense against some unseen danger.

On his way out, Eugenio had swiped her two week's pay and felt it a bargain.

Out on the street, The Spires still stretched into the heavens, but the floating counters and seats now rested on the floor, ostensibly to save power Eugenio thought. Still the doorwoman stood behind the plexi, her uniform just as creased and conservative. She seemed to recognize him and walked to the entrance, almost as if she'd been waiting for him. She opened the door before he reached it.

"Mr. McClaren left this for you," she said, holding out a palmlock key.

"Left this?" Eugenio asked.

"Yeah, even he left." She walked out the door and toward the parking garage, not bothering to say goodbye.

❖ ❖ ❖

When Eugenio stepped out of the elevator and through the anteroom of Mr. McClaren's penthouse, the view was amazing, but the contents of a small case on the kitchen counter took Eugenio's breath away. Inside he found the virtu rig that Mr. McClaren had promised, along with a wealth of files that detailed not just the transmission of the virus, but how the nanocells themselves triggered the disease to cause biocells to mutate and degrade.

With the evidence safely in hand, Eugenio strode over the plexi and looked out on the city. Just then the electricity in the surrounding blocks came back on, twinkling faintly in the chaos. He called Lucine and made plans to meet back up with her.

19

Rory nearly cried when he saw the Gardens. He hadn't remembered them this way: the quiet radiating out from the trees as golden light fell through the leaves in patches, and the overwhelming orange and purple blossoms that were bunched in semi-circular banks of fragrant blooms that melded with the smell of earth. He could barely see at all now, but felt grateful for what he could. If there were birds moving in this landscape, it would look less like a painting, but Rory delighted in its otherworldliness, as if his fantasies had come alive. It could not have been so lovely when he lived amongst people. He barely remembered the Gardens at all, just a rush of green as the train sped past on a drunken night and not much else.

"You gonna puke or something?" the rude girl said.

If he felt any better he'd love to shut her up, but as it was Rory ignored her and took in the green, the scent of flowers on the breeze. He could look forever at the Gardens it seemed. They held his attention even more than the streets. He saw the debris of the people that had left, heard the errant shot or yell, but all of this didn't darken his mood. Physically, he felt horrendous. The numbness was gradually being replaced by searing pain. Breathing became harder with each breath. Soon his legs might buckle and thirst plagued him. But still he felt amazed, reborn, rewarded. He stood outside, among people, touching them, and so no one could tell Rory that anyone anywhere was luckier than him.

"Let's go back to the corner," the rude girl said.

"Back to the corner?" Rory's girl replied. She still wouldn't tell him her name, not that he cared terribly at the moment. Apparently Starlings, like virtuosos, hid their identities.

"Or out to The Shallows. Have a drink or a smoke," she offered.

"Or to Dannel's for some new handhelds," one of the little ones said.

"—And digis," the tall boy said.

"Yeah, we've not looted nearly enough," someone else added.

"It's fucking boring after a while," Rory's girl said.

Rory took in the details of the deserted block next to the Gardens. Further down he saw droves of people walking west. He and the Starlings had been moving that direction but had split from the crowd at the Gardens.

"A fine day out for Rory of Yore," he said quietly.

"As I said, he's babbling now," rude girl said.

He wished that the girl could meet a virtuoso. Peru could show her what a proper smart-ass sounded like. She was the only person he wished to see on his great adventure, but still no answer. He didn't imagine she'd be the sort to abandon ship over the likes of some birds, or even the riots, but perhaps she too had left for fear of getting trapped here, or doing without the finer amenities. After a dozen years of linking into her reals, he didn't really know her well enough to say.

❖ ❖ ❖

By that afternoon, Rory couldn't open his eyes anymore. They'd swollen completely shut. He had to rely solely on sounds to take in the world. The tall boy had helped him adjust his hearing aids. He could hear their voices, but they seemed to be coming from a great distance. Talking also now seemed out of the question. Thankfully he could still drink. Rory's girl, though he started calling her Josette in his mind, had fashioned a straw contraption to go past his swollen tongue and straight to his throat. Rory choked as the water ran down his windpipe, but it quenched his parched throat.

They sat, he thought, at a bar. He could smell liquor and the remnants of smoke; he definitely remembered the sound of breaking glass before two of the Starlings helped him through the door.

He thought they should probably try to call for a medical unit and leave him here. Unfortunately Rory had thought of this only after talking became an insurmountable obstacle. And just at this moment he didn't care; though he might want to pass off his valuables to Josette just in case. For the moment, he sat in the steadily warmer room, listening hungrily to everything around him.

"A/C's kicked," someone said.

Rory's girl replied, "A/C's about kicked everywhere. We'll have to go lower."

"Or into the water," someone else replied.

This caught his attention. Once, he'd nearly fallen into the water just outside the Shallows train station. He'd been trying to illegally procure a special purple globe for one of his nieces; when he lost his footing, Rory found himself hanging on to the handrail. Not that he had been in any danger of drowning. The water in The Shallows had earned its name. But it could have very well been a social death of sorts—for most people.

Hanging there, he'd already thought of a new line or two to incorporate this into his seduction repertoire. He'd seen the look of fear and excitement on his niece's face and so Rory let go of the handrail, crashing into the water in the most acrobatic display he could improvise, splashing and flopping along the surface of the water. Thoroughly soaked, he leapt back up to the thoroughfare with the purple globe in hand, pinwheeling his arms and sending arcs of water streaming just in front of her. She squealed with delight and Rory basked in the beam of her smile.

Josette. If his mouth had worked, that's what he would have said: Josette, and Lisette. They would have been thirty and thirty-six. Perhaps married. Perhaps with their own children. Surely he would have been invited over for dinner, Rory thought.

"—downstairs. There's a wine cellar. We can rest down there until the A/C comes back online," Rory's girl said.

"Or the sun goes down," one of the boys replied.

Rory could feel the darkness as they descended down the stairs. It felt cool and moist and comforting; their steps echoed on the stone stairs underfoot, and as he moved the air seemed to slow and crystallize. Josette and the tall boy held him up as they came to rest at the bottom of the stairs, one under each arm.

In the time it must have taken their pupils to dilate, to drink in the darkness and wait for vision to emerge from it, Rory exhaled a last small breath, Josette's name on his lips.

20

Seife had said something, but Anna hadn't quite heard it. Noises from the city reached into Seife's home intermittently: an occasional yell, sirens, and others that Anna couldn't identify that made her most uneasy of all. With a conscious effort, Anna tore her attention away.

"I'm sorry. What did you say?" Anna asked.

"Why did you want the birds?" Seife repeated.

"I didn't—necessarily. I was just thinking of someone and it made me remember the birds," Anna answered.

"Who was this someone?" Seife asked.

Anna didn't respond.

"Too soon?" Seife asked.

"No," Anna said quickly. "It was years ago. And complicated."

"Too soon for us, I meant," Seife said.

"Oh, I don't know. . ."

"So you called one of those services? Is it true they have a cart where you can pick one out?" Seife asked.

"I didn't smuggle them or buy them in The Dire," Anna said.

Anna steeled herself and plunged ahead. "I made them."

It was clear from Seife's blank expression that she didn't believe her.

"I'm not lying." Anna stood and walked to the door, pausing only to say, "I'll be back."

Anna knew, no doubt, Seife must be weighing her words. She'd already given the woman ample reason to think her unhinged. Now it seemed she had no other choice. Usually, Anna would leave it at that, but now she wanted nothing less than to leave it at that.

It was dusk. The kilns were cooling, but Anna could still feel warmth radiating from them as she walked past to the small workshop on the edge of the drying plain. She heard a faint crash from somewhere further into the city and quickened her pace to the kiln. Here, Seife had showed her during her tour, the bone black was made. She climbed the stairs to the entrance and knocked on the door. A deep baritone answered and she entered.

A gray-haired man, tall and willowy, leaned over a table in the middle of the room. He laid the completed pieces of bone black in neat rows. On an adjacent table, strips of red paper waited to be rolled around the charcoal. Dark powder dusted the floor.

"Yes?" he said, looking up. "You're Seife's friend, aren't you? Can I help you with anything?"

"Yes, the charcoal, how much is it?" Anna asked.

"For Seife's friend, it's free." Anna gave him one of her rare smiles in exchange and returned to Seife's.

Anna hesitated outside Seife's door. She pulled off her dust-covered boots and ran her feet under the small spigot near the bottom of the door. For now, she couldn't hear the echoes of unrest from the city and savored this moment of quiet before she upended the world again. At her feet a pool of charcoal dust gathered and ran down the spaces between the deck flooring. She watched as the sullied water joined the black-stained sand under Seife's house, under every house in Smoketown's grove of homes. She dried her feet and stepped inside. Dusk had just settled outside the window, but inside it felt as still as the dead of night, with only Seife's hushed breathing and the hum of the ceiling fan. Seife stood in the kitchen pouring herself a glass of water. She turned casually to Anna.

"I'll show you." Anna pulled her drawing pad out of her bag and the fresh charcoal stick out of her pocket. "What's your favorite bird?" Anna asked.

"A hummingbird," Seife said, a question in her voice.

Anna smiled to herself. "Of course."

She took out her handheld and typed the word in, found a photo and began to sketch. Every few seconds she glanced up at Seife. As Anna finished she said, "Ready?"

Before Seife could answer the bird burst up from the page and flew to the red tablecloth. Seife scrambled to the other side of the room, back pressed up against the wall. Her wide-eyed stare shuffled between Anna and the bird until her breathing slowed. Slowly she slid down the wall, her knees pressed into her chest.

Anna stood and walked to the door where the humming-bird flitted. She placed her hand on the knob to open it and let the bird out.

"Wait," Seife said. With some effort she stood and approached the hummingbird. The bird darted over to the kitchen window, then back to the middle of the room. Seife followed its movements with her eyes. She seemed to have forgotten about Anna for the moment, and for this Anna felt grateful. Grateful that Seife hadn't walked past her and out the door, didn't look at her strangely or for the moment at all, Anna waited, hand on the doorknob, to see where this moment would turn.

The beating of the bird's wings was the only sound in the room. Dust motes glided through the slanted light coming through the window. Anna mustered her courage and turned to Seife directly, ready to say what she didn't know, but sure she should say something. When Anna looked she saw something in Seife, or the beginnings of it. She had been lucky. In Seife's slowly blossoming smile and her tentative steps to follow the bird around the room, Anna saw Seife's wonder.

Content that they were all still in the same room, Anna leaned against the door and watched. As Seife began to investigate the bird in earnest, it repeatedly darted away from her and hovered, Anna walked over to the bed and sat down, fascinated by their dance. She wondered if the bird knew of Seife's song. A silly thought—the first she could remember having in a very long time.

"It can't live in this room," Seife said finally and opened the kitchen window. She walked the few meters to the bed and sat down next to Anna. They both watched the hummingbird's departure.

"Unbelievable," Seife said, turning to Anna. "You created a life. You see? I was right. You are different."

Anna thought, this is the accident of attraction. It wasn't that Seife had given her a place to stay when there was no place left for her in the world, the mornings she'd spent listening to her voice echo through the city, or the truths that Seife had shared with her. It was simply the way Seife looked at her when she finished speaking that broke Anna's hard-won reserve. She turned to Seife and kissed her with a softness that Anna didn't know had survived in her.

Slowly, Anna dragged her fingers back from where she held Seife's jaw and closed her hand in a loose ball. She waited for the call of Seife's flesh to stop echoing, to forget the exquisiteness of her skin long enough to collect her own thoughts and whisper soft words that would allow the moment to settle gently, so that they could come back to it. She did not want this something between them to burst.

"I should go," Anna said, more out of reactionary fear than sincerity. She couldn't remember the last time anyone had been so close.

Seife said nothing, kept watching Anna steadily as the breeze that ruffled the leaves outside the window. The faintest aroma of smoke wafted in, momentarily dividing Anna's attention.

Anna said with more certainty, "I should go." She paused. "At least to the couch."

"Should you?" Seife asked.

"Yes," Anna answered.

"Will you?"

Anna smiled and started to get up, thought better of it and turned back to Seife. The kiss almost made her forget and with a sustained effort she pulled away.

"Goodnight, Seife."

"Sleep here tonight," Seife said.

Anna lay in Seife's bed in the warm crook of the other woman's arm and though the disjointed pieces of her felt closer, her trepidation hadn't disappeared. The ache in her legs faded; the soreness in her back was forgotten; her headache abated, but still the gnawing in her chest remained. For now Anna rested.

21

On the morning of the evacuation's second day, Eugenio and Lucine sat inside the perimeter's last circuit station, Post Eight. They'd had a minor scare when they met back up at Post Six, a sentry who they thought had actually stayed at his station, but as it turned out he'd just been retrieving the post's wheeled extinguishers to help fight the fires. They'd watched him load up the haul and disappear toward the blazes in the center of the city.

Now Eugenio watched as Lucine took a velveteen roll out of her pack and placed it in front of the final panel, slowly unrolling it toward the east to reveal the small collection of picks, skeleton keys, blades, and rounded adzes that she'd carefully fashioned from her best finds at The Dumps. Lucine had spent the last three years finding and fashioning the half-dozen tools. The top half of each tool stuck out of the fabric. She began with the long thin pick that had been a microphone coil in its former life.

She worked quickly, familiar now with this work. Eugenio, too, had grown accustomed to the tasks she'd assigned to him. Carefully, he removed the face of the drive motor and looked for the yellow wire she'd be needing next.

He could hardly believe they were so close to success. Lovely, magnetic Lucine had drawn together all the pieces to complete their task, even bringing him back to himself long enough to stay the course. In his pack Rory's virtu rig would finish the job they started today. Eugenio felt the corners of his mouth rise into a smile.

The last post was easy enough to dismantle. Lucine shorted out the circuit, and disassembled the power matrix. She and Eugenio went outside to cut the lines for backup power. He eyed the mound of dead birds on the outside of the perimeter, piled up against the invisible barrier. Two fat vultures stood atop the mound, feeding. Eugenio looked away and over to Lucine crouched over the backup box dug into the earth. She pulled out the last relay, and the omnipresent hum stopped. For a second the silence overtook Eugenio, and he remembered how quiet the city had once been. He closed his eyes, savoring the memory and the return of that quiet. A second later, the mound of birds toppled over into the now empty space. When it finally settled the mound resembled a narrowing path pointing back into Leiodare.

The city looked the same as it had this morning—The Spires reaching up, The Dumps in the east, a dead space above and below. It did not feel the same though, that had changed instantly.

A black bird flew toward them. They watched as it flew up and out. With sudden clarity, Eugenio realized there was no more 'out'. Lucine clapped. Eugenio could not move; a knot of emotion lodged itself in his throat. The souls he had seen last night could now be free. This was just the first. He watched the black bird reach the surrounding jungle, the clouds, and what lay beyond. Within seconds, more birds took to the sky, flowing in and out of the city.

"Eu," Lucine said, as she began to pack up her tools. "Did you see that?"

She made it as far picking up the cutters before she, like her brother, could only sit and watch the sky.

22

They must have lain in bed for nearly a day because when Anna's eyes opened and her gaze drifted to the window, she saw the soft light of dusk and another distant glow beyond it. The faint smell of smoke mixed with the scent of Seife's skin. Not yet ready to give up this moment of hard-fought peace, she closed her eyes. Anna felt Seife's breath warm her ear, the comfort of Seife's arms around her and scooted back until they touched. She could not remember the feeling of being held and hadn't realized its absence had carved into her until this moment when there was someone to fill that space.

Sudden banging on the front door jerked Seife awake.

"What the . . . ?" she muttered behind Anna. Seife dragged herself out of bed. Anna rolled over onto her suddenly bare back and sat up, watching Seife make her way to the door.

"Enough!" Seife said, a few steps from the entrance. She flung the door open and Anna saw Seife's brother Rene, out of breath, filling up the doorway. Makisig was barely visible just behind him.

"The fires are spreading," Rene said.

"Where?" Seife asked.

"Here, or on their way. A quarter of the Gardens are gone. The winds have picked up. They're strong," Rene answered. "We're digging a fire line. Can you help?"

"Of course," Seife answered, putting on her shoes. Anna, already out of bed, met them at the door. On the landing, she put on her boots and they hurried down to Rene's trans.

Outside a thick haze had already begun to infiltrate the neighborhood.

"Everyone else is already there. Those who can help anyway. Jai Ling is rounding up the kids and older folks for an evac, in case."

The distant glow Anna had seen outside Seife's bedroom window grew bright orange as the trans drew closer to the rest of the city. Rene drove over the last rise in Smoketown and Anna could see the fire's full intensity—she had never seen anything like it.

There were only two colors here: orange and black. The city and the Gardens had become a place of shadows and flame, where the live things, even the people in the trans, already seemed to have crossed over into darkness. Air had been replaced by smoke and night had become a bright, hot landscape where conflagrations of fire popped up every hundred meters. The trans' cooling motor grew loud as it tried to offset the heat beating into the passenger cabin. It looked to Anna like the individual fires were close to merging. As they drove slowly on, a line of shadow people digging into the dirt became visible in the murk. Makisig pulled wet handkerchiefs out of a compartment in the floorboards and handed one to each of them.

"The last of the goggles," he said, distributing those as well.

"Okay," Rene said, opening the door. The roar of the fire immediately enveloped them. He opened the trunk. Anna saw Rene's mouth moving but couldn't quite understand what he said. Seife handed her a pick from the back of the trans and they joined the others at the end of the line. On the third swing of the pick, a tree thirty meters from Anna ignited.

"The winds are shifting," Rene yelled. Another man further down the line yelled something, but Anna couldn't hear what it was. The people nearest him abandoned their work and ran. The man hurried over to them.

"It's creating these winds, must be jet stream," he coughed out. "Firestorm. Can't be fought. Have to evac. Now."

Anna turned to Seife just in time to see a fire whirl, tall as a tower, two hundred meters away dancing back and forth. It turned east to west and back again, carving a path of destruction back into the city center. The man followed her gaze.

"There will be more. We have to leave," he said.

Rene, Makisig, and Seife began to move back to the trans. Anna brought up the rear. When they reached the trans, she closed the door behind Seife.

"I'll meet you back," Anna said.

"What? What are you talking about? Get in the trans."

"I'll meet you back. I can do something about this," Anna answered.

Rene opened the door and got out, Anna was sure with every intention of picking her up and throwing her inside.

"Rene," Anna said calmly. "Get back in and get out of here." Something shifted in the wind. Anna stopped moving and closed her eyes. There. It felt like the slightest pull in the air. It would happen soon. She had to do something.

"Fuck," Anna said. She glared at Rene with an intensity that stopped him. He looked uncertainly over at Seife.

"Get him. Inside. And go," Anna said. The fire would soon suck everything into its center. They couldn't run from it, and Smoketown wouldn't survive it. Anna knew it as clearly as she knew that everyone, Seife, Rene, the refugees from the city, and perhaps even more would die in a matter of minutes if she did nothing.

"Get in," Seife said to her brother, though her gaze stayed locked on Anna. "You need to be right about this."

Rene didn't move.

"Get in!" Seife yelled. With hesitation, Rene got back in his trans, staring at Anna as he did. Finally he shook his head and they sped off.

What could she use? What? Everything around her would burn.

"Goddammit," Anna spat, trying to think. Think back to organic chem—nothing. Inorganic then. Flame-resistant compounds. What did she have around her? There was phosphorous and nitrogen in the fertilizer, calcium silicate from the road. It would have to do. She would have to project; she had never tried it. But there was no time and nothing else. This would hurt.

Anna clenched her jaw and dropped down to the road. Immediately the skin on her lower legs began to hurt. She drew the structure with her hands, shaping what she wanted in the air until she could see its beginning and end, the vision as clear as she could make it. She reached out and placed one palm on the road and one on the mineral-rich earth next to it. Anna could barely see through the smoke and so closed her eyes.

She concentrated on the essence of what she wanted to create, holding the vision of the dome that would contain the fire, and for once, hoped she had it in her to do. The pain in her hands throbbed up her arms; she smelled her hair beginning to burn, and when she opened her eyes she saw the very tips beginning to curl in on themselves. Anna had to finish quickly. The pain would become too much and she'd lose the ability to focus. Turning her gaze up, she saw that a dark glimmering sheen, like low tide, had spread from her hands, across the ground and now rose fifty meters into the air. Closing her eyes, she willed every part of her and every atom at her disposal to push, to build before the road beneath her burst into flame or the fire sucked them all into its heart. The skin on her hand blistered and burned. She felt soon it would melt.

Anna screamed in agony. As she did she felt a force move through her, and burst out, both pain and, bizarrely, pleasure. It sucked the air from her lungs and she fell over sideways into the dirt. For an instant her hands stuck, then broke from the road and ground as if they'd been freed from ice. She opened her eyes to see the dome reach further up than she could see. Inside it the fire roared. With each breath, its flames shrank and the smoke inside thickened until Anna could see nothing inside, only the moon above it, now shining softly as the winds began to clear away the fumes.

She lay there until the fire had burned itself out. Just before she fainted, Anna saw Seife appear above her, her expression full of concern, dreadlocks haloing her face.

23

Eugenio leaned against the railing of the Texico City iCDC office, watching Lucine cross the avenue to join him. The sunglasses she wore resembled a virtu rig, but underneath she wore a relaxed expression, her limbs moving languidly as she walked.

A recent rain had dampened the dust that usually swirled around this part of Texico City. Eugenio pulled down the cloth he'd tied around his mouth earlier and rubbed his hand over the stubble on his jaw. Perhaps they could take some time to regroup now—or at least shave. They'd delivered his transcripts, Rory's files, and the Series 3 rig safely to the office. ICDC and their governing body now could decide how to handle the City Health Department and file proper charges against McClaren Industries. Unfortunately, Rory wouldn't witness any of that. His body had been found in The Shallows a week ago. Still Eugenio thought he might have received some satisfaction, and because Rory had helped expose the truth perhaps the company would be judged separately from the family. Eugenio would work toward that end when he and Lucine returned.

Emergency Management had finally reintroduced some control and suppressed the small band of diehard Starlings whose blackout rampage caused most of the chaos. Now Eugenio and Lucine could help rebuild.

The broadcast images showed that those few days had cost the city dearly—but The Spires still stood, also a limited number of buildings in the Center, and The Shallows had been largely untouched. Most fortunately, there were almost no casualties as most of the city had been on its way out when the worst hit. HQ centers had been set up in the Center and out in Smoketown. There would be enough to do, though Eugenio still wasn't sure in what capacity he would do it. Emergency Management had promoted Lena to the Director's job and offered him hers. Eugenio doubted he wanted to spend much time behind a desk, but ornithophobia wouldn't go away because the perimeter had. Perhaps he could have a hand in creating a municipal treatment program.

A massive billboard lumbered past, blocking the view with an image of breakfast cereal.

An alert chime sounded from his handheld. He removed it from his pocket and tapped the flashing alarm icon.

"It's time?" Lucine said, closing the last few meters between them.

"Yes, the broadcast should be hitting Leiodare now as well."

The image on the billboard blacked out. The logo for a newscast replaced it. Breaking News flashed across the board. An immense head appeared on the board. Eugenio marveled at the size of the man's face. The image's pores were as big as Eugenio's hands.

"An ion blast from the iCDC HQ: Sources have confirmed that the agency has received compelling evidence that the Crumble superbug was the result of corporate negligence. McClaren Industries, maker of the once-omnipresent virtu and Last Word systems, is alleged to be behind the epidemic. Viewers may recall that thirty years ago McClaren Industries revolutionized the entertainment industry with the introduction of virtu systems. While a steady stream of competitors went on to take over the market, McClaren Industries remains a substantial player in virtu systems. And at the time of the Crumble McClaren Industries had ninety-eight percent market share within the city. How's that for irony?"

Eugenio's stomach turned at the broadcaster's flippancy.

"Charges have been filed for corporate espionage, criminal negligence, fraud, and—" His tone became incredulous. "A count of premeditated murder! The company and several former staff stand accused of the murder-for-hire of a nanotech named Bly Ori, who apparently stumbled on their secret first. One of her colleagues is with us today." The broadcaster shifted his gaze. "Dr. Khan, thank you for your time. What can you tell us about Bly Ori?" he asked. The billboard showed an older woman with dark curls and a kind face.

"She was a dedicated and extremely talented researcher and designer, the Lee Dalton of her time. Her work was remarkable. Truly remarkable. Until her retirement she led the field," Dr. Khan said.

"Yes, you bring up an interesting point. McClaren Industries is accused of having her murdered—after she had retired. Can you give us any insight on that?"

"I'm afraid I can't. But I can tell you that she left the lab on maternity leave, and while gone decided to retire. It's not uncommon, though rare for a tech of her skill level and at that point in her research."

"Exactly what kind of research was she engaged in?" he asked.

"I can't divulge those details, as the work is the exclusive property of Note Labs. But I can tell you if Bly had had the opportunity to fully develop her work it would've been of great benefit to the world," she said.

"Hmm, a loss for us all then—courtesy of McClaren Industries," the broadcaster said, turning directly to the audience. "This has been a Vivant Industries bulletin. Have a vibrant day."

The cereal bowl flashed back on-screen.

"It's the message that matters, Eu," Lucine said.

"Yes, it is," Eugenio said, stepping away from the railing. "Did you send word about the freed souls?" he asked.

"To every Mendejano receiver in the south and east. They'll move it along its way. I also let them know that the perimeter won't be rebuilt," she said proudly. She reached up and squeezed his shoulder. "This is a good start to your histories, Eu."

"Thank you."

"But just a start."

He laughed. "Let's go home."

24

"Bly" was all Anna heard. She sat on Seife's couch, ankles crossed, watching the news broadcast on her handheld when her mother's name stopped time. Anna paused the broadcast, and disbelieving, rewound the report three times before understanding sunk down and settled inside her. "They" had a name, and they had not killed Bly for her gifts. They probably didn't even know about them. And someone who may have, by what she insinuated in the interview, had never betrayed her mother, even all these years later.

Despite the shock of seeing her mother's story, Anna didn't black out or lose time. The room shimmered and warped—but after that moment passed, she still found herself on the couch, aching from the blisters on her hands, alone. Anna got up and went to find Seife. Anna knew Seife was either out helping to destroy the dome or near the drying plains assisting with the bird burial.

Gingerly, Anna got up from the couch and went out into the day. Outside, cool air prickled the flesh of her arms as she descended the stairs and crossed the short clearing into the undergrowth. Not yet sure how to start the story she had to tell, her gaze flitted over the trees, the sunlight in the leaves, the pods fluttering down into her path. Distracted by their flight she didn't notice the woman walking her way. When Anna did, she flicked her gaze over to the woman, and lost the rhythm of her steps.

Peru.

She saw Peru, alive, walking toward her through the jungle. Anna started to open her mouth—to say what, she wasn't sure—when the other woman's face rippled and changed. As the woman emerged from the shadows between trees, Anna saw full lips and high cheekbones—even her skin appeared darker, caramel where there had been cream. Anna's memory flashed an image of the girl in the real, standing in the Idahoan desert. She almost expected the woman coming toward her to smile and wave. Peru was showing off now as she'd done then.

As she slowly closed the distance between them, Anna finally saw Peru for what and who she was—the product of Bly's blood and nanocells, capable of changing herself at will, but a woman so incapable of change that she had faked her own death to be left alone.

Anna was not responsible for what Peru did in the world and could certainly not control her. If she owed Peru anything, it was gratitude for this last harsh lesson.

When they neared each other, Anna held out one hand, stopping Peru. She turned and looked at the other woman full in the face. Anna had grown since they last met, or perhaps Peru had shrunk. However it had happened, she could now look Peru in the eye.

"*This* is what you'll do to be left alone," Anna said.

"It is," Peru's gaze stayed fixed on the trees in front of her. "You surprised me though—with the birds. I didn't think you were listening back then."

"I always listened, I just didn't always understand."

An aracari's song filled the silence. Peru looked over at Anna.

"You can't be you know—alone," Anna said, turning to her. She thought of her mother and the path that had brought her here. "And even if you think you are, you're always alone with something—your fear, guilt. If you're lucky—." Anna scanned Peru's new face. "Yourself."

Slowly, Anna let her hand drop to her side, and looked out towards the jungle.

"I always wanted to ask you, why 'Peru'? The name I mean."

"It was the first word I recognized," Peru answered.

Anna grunted softly. "That's so much simpler than the scenarios I'd come up with."

"You tend to complicate things, Anna."

Anna couldn't help but smile. She turned back to Peru. "I did. But it's time to let some things die and new ones live."

With that, Anna continued on her way, leaves crunching loudly underfoot.

about the author

Tenea D. Johnson was born in Louisville, Kentucky. Fifty years before that, her paternal grandparents met there, in a neighborhood called Smoketown. She received her BA from New College of Florida and her MA from NYU's Gallatin School. She has written a poetry and prose collection, Starting Friction. Her shorter work has appeared in various anthologies and magazines; her musical work, compositions of storytelling to music, are available on disc and online. She currently lives near the Gulf of Mexico under the canopy of a centuries-old oak (in a house). This is her first novel.

Also Available from Blind Eye Books

The Archers Heart
Books One, Two & Three
by Astrid Amara

Two Tangled Tales
by Astrid Amara

Turnskin
by Nicole Kimberling

Wicked Gentlemen
by Ginn Hale

Lord of the White Hell
Books One & Two
by Ginn Hale

The Rifter Series
Books One—Ten
by Ginn Hale

Feral Machines
by Ginn Hale

Strange Fortune
by Josh Lanyon

For more information go to blindeyebooks.com
or weightlessbooks.com